PUF

The

Will Gatti has been a warehouse man, van driver, children's book editor, and a teacher. He has lived in France and the west coast of Ireland where he set his first novel. He now lives in Surrey with his wife and two children where he teaches English and writes.

The
Drowning Pool

Will Gatti

PUFFIN BOOKS

PUFFIN BOOKS

Published by the Penguin Group
Penguin Books Ltd, 27 Wrights Lane, London w8 5TZ, England
Penguin Books USA Inc., 375 Hudson Street, New York, New York 10014, USA
Penguin Books Australia Ltd, Ringwood, Victoria, Australia
Penguin Books Canada Ltd, 10 Alcorn Avenue, Toronto, Ontario,
Canada M4V 3B2
Penguin Books (NZ) Ltd, 182–190 Wairau Road, Auckland 10, New Zealand

Penguin Books Ltd, Registered Offices: Harmondsworth, Middlesex, England

First published in Puffin Books 1997
1 3 5 7 9 10 8 6 4 2

Set in 11/14 Linotron Sabon
Typeset by Rowland Phototypesetting Ltd,
Bury St Edmunds, Suffolk
Made and printed in England by Clays Ltd, St Ives plc

British Library Cataloguing in Publication Data
A CIP catalogue record for this book is available from the British Library

ISBN 0-140-38311-5

FOR THOMAS AND GEORGIA

CHAPTER ONE

I am ten.

I sometimes wish I was a boy. I know that it's silly to wish for things that can't happen but I do anyway, like wishing that Dad hadn't gone away and that I could talk to Peter sometimes; and that maybe I wasn't me but somebody else. I think that's what Mum wishes.

'Why can't you make friends? Don't you know how?'

I don't know why – I don't do it on purpose.

I hate it when Mum cries; her face goes all slippery and she gets embarrassed and tries to smile, and I hate that. I don't think boys cry very much. I don't cry at all.

I'm not particularly bad but I do tell, well, not lies exactly, but they just slip out . . . I suppose they are lies. I am not ten; I am eleven.

I'll tell you something else about me. I used to pray all the time for a bit but I've stopped because it didn't work, and now I've decided to be a witch instead. Witches, I know for a fact, can make things happen.

They don't have friends either – except their cats – but that doesn't bother me. I won't make any friends in my new home, whatever Mum says. Anyway I don't want friends because I don't like talking to people, and that's why I hate school because people keep talking to you the whole time. Mum says the village school I'm going to is nice and that I will like it. I won't.

Poor Mum, she gets practically everything wrong, which is why I don't want to be like her when I grow up. You know, it scares me not knowing what I'll turn into when I'm older. What happens if I become something I really hate? How can you stop that happening? I don't know, but what I have done is this: I have made a list of all the things I don't want to become. The trouble is I am bound to lose it. I'm not stupid but I do lose everything. If I did have friends I would probably lose them straight away. So what *is* going to happen? I'll grow up, look for the list, not be able to find it and then BANG! I'll turn into a mother who spends all her time crying and wanting her little daughter to be something she is not.

'We're nearly there, Kate.'

She says she's worried about uprooting me from London and all that. I don't mind. One place is probably the same as another. And as for uprooting! I mean it's not as if I'm a tree or anything.

She keeps turning the radio on and off and tapping her fingers on the wheel and looking in the mirror the whole time. There isn't anything behind us except a long line of cars crawling away into the distance, like so many beetles.

Mum's hair looks a bit like a beetle's back, a glossy black blob. She had it cut short just before we left. I don't like it much but I didn't tell her that. It's best not to tell the truth sometimes. She is nice looking though, even with her hair like this. I like the way she dresses too: she often wears jeans and a floppy old suede jacket with a pink paint blob on the sleeve. The jacket was Dad's. She told me she bought it for him, but I never remember him wearing it. She got paint on it because she gets paint on everything. At least, she used to when she painted. She hasn't done any pictures for ages.

'You're not making faces out of the back window, are you, Kate?'

'No.' I am of course. So's Rabbit. But it's Mum's fault for looking in the mirror the whole time; it made me wonder whether anyone was following us.

Rabbit, I had better tell you, is a fluffy glove puppet. Well, he *was* fluffy; he's a bit bare in places now. And it's no good telling me I'm too old for cuddly toys because Rabbit isn't really a cuddly toy. I don't cuddle him for one thing. He is just Rabbit and I feel odd if I don't have him with me. I talk to him sometimes. Mum says if I threw him away I would start to make friends which is stupid. Rabbit has nothing to do with whether I have friends or not.

*

We come off the motorway and pass through the outskirts of somewhere called Hereford. I looked it up on the map before we started. It's on the left. Mum points out a school I might be going to when I'm thirteen. I think the word 'glum' was invented to describe schools. Still this one, if I ever get to it or live that long, is not as bad as a large building called Our Lady's Home that we pass a little later which is *really* grim with huge black railings all round it, and its name curved in iron letters over the main gate. The building is dark with tall pointed roofs. I don't see any people anywhere. Mum says she thinks it's a hospital for the mentally ill. I show it to Rabbit.

The closer we get to our village the more she keeps telling me how it's so good to have green things all around and how she's never lived in the country before but has always wanted to.

If she always wanted to live in the country, she and Dad shouldn't have bought a house in London. Everything might have been different if we had been living in the country.

'Here we are! Isn't it pretty?'

The village is called Bexstead-under-Wood, which I have to admit is a good name. And there *are* woods too. In fact, even before she said that we'd arrived I was aware of the trees – a great wall of them off to our right as we were driving along, deep and green. I thought I spotted a gypsy camp too. I think I like the idea of living near gypsies.

Then we cross over a humpy bridge by some fields and we are in the main street. Mum is right; it is pretty. The houses are mostly white with black beams and bulging walls that look as if they've got toothache. There's a green, and an old-looking church with a funny gate that has a roof over it.

I find myself hoping that our house is one of these twisty, little buildings and I keep expecting her to stop and say this is it, but we keep going until we reach the edge of the village. There, sandwiched between a paddock with two dim-looking horses in it and the wood, is a collection – that doesn't sound right – a bundle, a scrumble of new houses all plopped down together.

'This is it!'

It's an estate: Underwood Close. It's so new that some of the houses haven't even been finished and the pavement isn't made up yet. There are mixers and piles of sand dumped on the corners (which aren't really corners but bendy curves). We wind our way into it. There are about twenty houses, perhaps not so many, and they're all empty too. 'Is everyone dead?'

'Don't be silly.' She slows so that she can peer at the house numbers. 'I thought a few other families might have moved in by now. John said there'd been a lot of interest in the development. Still,' she adds brightly, 'we're the first. That's something isn't it?'

Perhaps it is.

Uncle John is what Mum calls a property developer, which means he makes lots of money and builds lots of houses. He and Dad used to work together. Dad is an architect; designs houses and things. You have to be incredibly clever to be an architect. 'If Dad had designed this estate, there would be people living in it.' Mum pretends not to hear. She and Dad are divorced.

We come right to the end and there is our house – small, neat, white and with a long front lawn that runs right down to the wood. We really are underwood! I like that. I also like the way we have our back to the rest of the estate. I'll be able to look for mushrooms and toadstools here.

Suddenly Mum slams on the brakes and I bang forward into the back of her seat.

'What on earth do you think you're doing?'

For a second I think she's yelling at me and I am trying to think what it is I've done wrong. If I think hard enough I can usually find something.

I haul myself up, one hand over my nose to check that it's still pointing in the right direction, and I see this boy right up against the car. He's on a bike which looks about three sizes too big for him, and he's keeping his balance by holding on to the bonnet. He's very scruffy with red, curly hair; orangey-red like fire, and his elbows are sticking out of a black pullover. 'Sorry, missus.' He doesn't sound bothered at all.

'I should think so. I could have killed you.' Mum

is still cross. 'Now do you mind getting out of the way?'

He acts like he hasn't heard her. 'You come here to live 'ave you?' He's looking at me when he asks this and I nod and then realize I have my hand over my nose and snatch it away. He turns and gives Mum a big smile and says, 'Good luck then,' and twists his bike out of the way so that we can drive on.

Mum is thrown. She's no good if anyone is charming to her – no one apart from me that is. I used to try quite a lot and it only seemed to irritate her so I gave up. 'Well, he seemed nice.'

I hold up Rabbit so that he can look and see. The boy is still standing there, one foot on the ground, one on the pedal. Rabbit shakes his head; he doesn't look that nice.

We drive on a tiny bit to the gate of our new house and pull up again. There is a house a little further back on the estate road, on the opposite side to ours. It's also got a garden running down to the wood. It has a window broken to the right of the front door.

Our house even smells new. Our old house was nice; my bedroom had a slopey ceiling and looked over a canyon of gardens. There were always cats stalking along the wall which divided the gardens of the houses on our street from those which belonged to the houses of the next street.

We're having some things brought down by movers this afternoon; not that much though. I think she must have left a lot of her stuff behind, or just got rid of it. I think that if you have something you like, you should keep it for ever.

'Do you like it, Kate?' She sounds almost nervous but the truth is that, although the room she shows me – my room – is a box, it's fine and that's what I tell her. Like my old bedroom, this looks out on the garden but, even better, it looks right towards the wood.

'I hope you won't be lonely here, Kate.'

'I like being on my own.' The wood looks brilliant – witches, bandits, rabbits, the last of the Mohicans . . .

'Yes, of course.'

I'm quite pleased we moved. I didn't say this before but our London house had a sad feeling in it that would sometimes keep me awake at night.

We unpack, and have lunch. I have a sandwich; Mum smokes cigarettes, and then the movers arrive.

I go outside while they're scurrying backwards and forwards with our things, and the boy appears again. I see him watching from down the end of the street. I pretend not to take any notice of him. Then he comes racing towards me and at the last moment he yanks the front wheel off the road and skims along like that, until he skids to a stop just beside the removals lorry.

'Wheelie,' he says.

Although I would like to be a boy, I'm not really

impressed by things like wheelies. I don't say anything.

'What's your name?'

'Geoffrey,' I say. I told you, didn't I, that I say things just without thinking sometimes?

'You kidding?' I can see him sort of sizing me up. That's all right. I think I'm a bit bigger than him anyhow.

I shake my head. Geoffrey is a good name. I like it. 'You don't live in this estate, do you?'

'No. Other side of village.'

'What are you doing here?'

'Watching.' He looks like he wants to say something else but I don't feel like asking him anything more.

'Got a lot of stuff, haven't you?' The men are carrying in our piano. 'Are you rich?'

'No.'

He swings the bike round. 'Don't have much to say for yerself do you?'

I don't bother to answer that one. The boy rides off. Rabbit and I were right about him.

The phone is ringing when I go in. I leave her to answer it and I go up to my room and try to make it a bit mine, shifting the bed slightly, putting out my books and then I take out my photo album, the one with the picture of Peter and me in it. Peter is four and he's got a cap on and it's tilted a bit to one side and his socks are down round his ankles. He's looking serious; he did a lot of the time, even when he was being funny. And I'm standing beside him, holding his hand. I love that picture.

A little bit later we have our first visitor – a lady in a blue anorak who Mum says is from the social services but I notice a police car up at the corner. She shows Mum her card and they go into the kitchen. I'm not allowed in but I try to listen at the door. I hear Mum saying 'Oh my God!' but she's always saying that. The radio's on in the background which makes it difficult to hear properly.

When the woman goes, Mum gives me a huge lecture about not going into the wood for the time being. 'Absolutely not at all, Kate.' She is very serious.

I find it wiser to say yes at times like this; arguing only leads to rows and doors being slammed. But not go into the wood? She must be mad.

Something wakes me in the night. I get up and look out of the window. It's so quiet here, no cars, nothing, and so dark I can't see the trees, just this deep black hump against the darkness. I go back to bed wondering what it was that woke me. I dream about Peter.

CHAPTER TWO

Do you ever want to be someone else? A witch can fix things like that; you want to be a lion, BANG! And there you are, mouth as big as a dustbin . . . The trouble with witches in stories is that they're not very clever; just to show off, they turn themselves into something little and then get eaten. I'm sure real witches are much smarter. Anyway, who wants to be turned into an animal? I don't. Though to tell the truth, there was a time when I wanted to be a dog, but that was ages ago.

But I would like to be different; in a different family maybe — and I would have long legs and knees that didn't look like tennis balls, and hair that was shiny. I'd still be a witch, of course, but I would hardly ever have to do any magic.

I don't really like to talk about Peter, not about what happened, but it's stupid to make a fuss about something that's over and done with. That's what Mum says. It's just that sometimes it doesn't feel as if it is over. Anyway, Peter is my brother. Or should I say 'was'? Does someone stop being your brother because they are dead? I don't know.

He died four years ago. I was seven. He had blond,

curly hair, and blue eyes, and socks that were always down around his ankles like in the photo I have of him; and he was everyone's pet; but you couldn't help liking him anyway. When he got cross he used to crouch behind the fridge and growl like a lion. That was Peter. He would be eight now.

It was my fault he died. Dad, Peter and me were out shopping. Dad went into a pub to buy cigarettes. He was in there for ages and I got bored. He told me to hold Peter's hand and not move, but you see he was in there for such a long time and there was a pet shop on the other side of the road. It was the time I was going through my dog bit and the pet shop had pups in the window. It wasn't just me, Peter wanted to go and look in the window too. I don't know how it happened because I didn't let go of his hand and I did look right and left, but when we ran there was suddenly this car hooting and he must have let go then. Then there was a terrible squealing and a thump and people shouting, and I was on the pavement and Peter wasn't beside me any longer.

I don't remember exactly what happened then, just people everywhere and Dad crying in the middle of the road, and being cross with me in front of everyone, and Peter bundled up at his feet. All I could see was his blue mac and his blond hair. I didn't see his face. There was an ambulance and then they whisked him off to hospital, but I think he was killed straight away.

Mum and Dad never said anything to me about it after that, but they argued with each other all the time. I mean they fought, screams and yelling up and down the stairs till I thought it was normal for families to be like that, and then eventually all that stopped but it wasn't any better because they stopped talking to each other altogether. Completely. Not even, 'Pass me the sugar.'

When I was eight, Dad left home. I haven't seen him for three years. I miss him, I think, but I miss Peter more and think about him most of the time.

I get funny feelings about Peter occasionally, that he's so close that if I just half-turned my head he'd be there, but he never is. That's why I said he 'is' my brother because it's as if he hasn't completely gone away yet. I want to see him again so I can say sorry. I'd hate to think of him always hiding somewhere near me, growling.

You probably won't believe this but when I woke up this morning I was sure he was in the room. I knew that when I opened my eyes he'd be gone, so I lay there with my eyes shut, holding Rabbit tight and concentrating, wishing he would say something.

Then Mum breezed in, pulled open the curtains, and that spoilt everything. It's not her fault I suppose, she just tends to be a breezy sort of person sometimes.

'What's this?'

The trouble with a new house is that you don't have secret places to hide things. Mum had picked up my private photograph album that I always keep hidden but which I left out last night.

I give her my worst scowl. I don't look so nice when I scowl. I don't look particularly nice when I don't scowl because of my serious face. A pokey face with straight black hair that flops down from the top of my head and which won't stay back properly, even when I put it in a pony tail. That's me. And when I scowl my eyes go squinty and my mouth tightens up like it's been zipped shut. I know exactly what I look like because I sometimes check my scowl in the mirror to see if I can improve it.

'The picture, Kate. This one.'

'Oh.'

'Where did you get it?'

'Don't know.' I found it the day Dad packed to leave. He wasn't supposed to start packing until Mum had taken me out for a walk, but he did and I saw the suitcase. I knew what was going on; I'm not as stupid as they think I am. I went into the room. I don't remember where he was but he wasn't in there. I remember how neatly the case was packed, all his shirts folded like new ones are, and the photo was on the top. I took it and ran out of the room.

Mum was down in the hall shouting up at me to hurry up. I looked at her through the bannisters, then I slipped the photo between two books in the book-case on the landing. Nobody ever mentioned anything about the photograph as far as I know. Perhaps Dad thought Mum had taken it. I kept it hidden. It was a funny thing about our house, we never had photographs up anywhere, only Mum's paintings.

'It's not a terribly good one of you is it?' I'm still scowling. It's *my* picture now and I don't want her to take it. She gives me a funny half-smile. 'I don't think I have a picture of you smiling, Kate.'

'Oh.'

She closes the album and puts it back on the table.

I wish we did talk about Peter sometimes; but we don't.

We have breakfast and Mum again says that on no account am I to go into the wood. She's mad if she thinks that I won't go. Then we spend the rest of the morning unpacking and sorting. At twelve Uncle John arrives to take us out to lunch. I must tell you about Uncle John because in a way he is the reason that we moved out of London and down to this house here.

Uncle John was Dad's business partner until Daddy got so sick he stopped working altogether – that was when the shouting at home was at its worst. I think that Uncle John took over the company but I don't really know. Anyway he used to drop round to see Mum from time to time. I think he used to give her advice about things. I remember them having long talks in the kitchen.

'Hello Kate,' he says when I open the door to him. He gives me a kiss and asks how I like the house and all that. I don't think we like each other much but I don't know why. He smells of pink soap and he is getting quite fat. Still, Mum says he's a great help to her so I am polite and ask him questions like Mum tells me to do.

He checks his watch against the hall clock, calls out: 'Come on Megs,' – that's what he calls her; Dad used to call her that too – 'get your skates on. Grand tour before lunch.'

Mum's voice drifts down from her room: 'Won't be a minute.'

He adjusts the hall clock and then goes to the open front door and looks across our scrappy garden to the wood – 'Such a waste of good land.' I'm not sure whether he's talking to me or not. Then Mum comes clattering down the stairs. 'A couple of things I want to show you before lunch,' he says.

'OK.'

We pile into the car; me in the back. The back seat of his car is huge. Sometimes I think the back of a car is the loneliest place in the world.

We leave the village behind us, cross the small river and pass a lopsided house with a great black wheel stuck to the outside, which Uncle John says is an old water mill. I hadn't noticed it when we drove in.

'Ripe for tarting up, that one. The place is a gold mine. What do you think, Megs?'

'Very pretty,' says Mum, the same as yesterday. 'Unspoilt.'

'Exactly. That's what makes it so good.'

'No, it doesn't.'

He laughs.

The road cuts into the edge of a wood. On the left the trees look huge, big gnarled branches hooking out towards the road with leafy hands like they might pull us in. On the right it is all a bit more open. The wood on the left is Old Wood, the one that runs right up to our back door. It *is* old – hundreds and hundreds of years – says Uncle John. I wonder who told him that.

I can almost see Robin Hood's men, outlaws, peering out at us, and then we slow down and suddenly there is a big space with a gypsy camp on the far side of a scrubby field. I can see about six caravans and one a little apart from the rest which is really proper, painted blue and gold with a round roof and a thin chimney poking up. I can see some people moving about, and a few children but they're a bit too far off to make out clearly.

The car stops. 'Mess isn't it?' says Uncle John. 'Now on this side . . .' He pulls the car round and there, almost opposite the camp, a great big bite has been taken out of the wood, leaving a brown scrawled-up mess of stumps and roots and machines; diggers mainly. There's a yellow box building, and around it all a high wire fence; barbed wire, like a prison. '. . . Masterson Developments. Five minutes from the village, fifteen minutes to the train and two hours to London. Exclusive country residences they'll be and we'll have people falling over themselves to buy. What do you think?'

'It looks ugly, John.'

'Course it does, you silly girl.' He lights one of his small cigars. 'Be fine when it's finished and we've got rid of the gypos . . .'

'What do you mean?'

'Don't worry, I'll make some good deal for them. We'll probably call the place Romany View!' I don't think he cares at all about the gypsies and they've probably been there for years and years.

We start off again and he drives us all the way round Old Wood so I can see how big it is and how it climbs up almost to the top of the hill which over-looks the village. Then, before circling back into the village, he actually drives us up that hill and through a wide, pillared gateway to a large, ivy-covered house. 'This is where the squire lives. Pretty grand, eh?'

The windows are dark and there are splotches of weed like green measles across the gravel driveway. There's an old man hooped over a garden fork watch-ing us from the far side of the lawn.

'What do you think, Megs?' He takes Mum's hand. 'I'm going to have it. The old feller is almost ready to sell, got him eating out of me hand, know what I mean?'

I wonder whether he means the man with the fork.

I can tell Mum is impressed from the way she isn't saying anything; she's sort of drinking it in. She described the feeling to me once; it's when she sees something she would really like to paint. It's because she is an artist really.

'Say the word, Megs, and it's all yours. Scout's honour.' She laughs. 'Look at the view,' he says and we all twist round. 'Spectacular, eh? The whole village.'

It's like being on top of the world. The village is tucked in at the foot of the hill, and the river winds off across green fields, and another stream snakes into it, and in the distance I can just make out the smudge of Hereford.

Mum smiles. 'Get thee behind me, Satan,' she murmurs.

He gives a short laugh. 'Well then.' He flicks the stub of his cigar out of the window. 'How about lunch?'

We have lunch in a country hotel and Uncle John orders champagne, and organizes Mum's life for her. I get the feeling that he organized us down to Bexstead. And now he's fixing her up with a job in an office he's opening in the village – 'Just to tide you over,' he says. He's off abroad somewhere soon he says so we won't be seeing that much of him.

Mum lets me sip some of her champagne but it goes up my nose and Uncle John doesn't think it's funny when I get a spluttering fit and the waiter comes over with a glass of water.

He drives us home but when Mum invites him in

for coffee, I slip out. 'Just up to the green,' I tell them but there's only one place I want to go, the forbidden wood.

I keep hearing this song that goes: 'My mother said, I never should, play with the gypsies in the wood.' I don't want to play with anyone.

CHAPTER THREE

The wood's so quiet I can't hear anything at all except for me. I am trying to walk like an American Indian but my feet keep crunching on old leaves and twigs, and my breathing sounds like a hundred dinosaurs because I sprinted this far in case Mum spotted me.

I can't imagine American Indians walking as slowly as this; it's really boring and they'd never have got any scalping done. Anyway, it's impossible to be silent. It feels like I'm walking in dry cornflakes. I bet even the smartest Indian couldn't be silent doing that. They probably didn't have the same sort of dead leaves and twigs in those days.

And don't think I'm making all this din because I'm fat; I'm not. I can still slide right under the sofa, except for my head. I never thought I had such a huge head until I tried the sofa trick and I couldn't even wedge my face underneath it. I have a sudden picture of me under the sofa with Mum and Uncle John sitting there, and my head is sticking out somewhere between their legs but they don't notice me. It's funny . . . and then somehow it's not such a nice thought. I don't know why.

It's odd not to hear anything except me; not a single

car, nothing, but perhaps that's good. If Peter does come back, I wonder how he will be. Will it be like I've just woken him?

After a bit the path forks. It's darker and cooler here. If I look up, the sun on the leaves makes them the colour of peppermint ice cream. Some of the trees are knobbly and out of the corner of my eye I can always see their half-faces peering at me. Trees can't hurt you.

The path ends in a little circle of trees and bushes. It's not exactly a fairy ring which is really what I wanted but it will do. I smooth out a space in the middle and then carefully sprinkle the salt I've pinched from the kitchen in a circle but there's not quite enough to go round, so I then spend ages taking pinches from the bit of the circle I've already made to try and fill in the circle, but the pinches are mainly dirt. I can't help the gaps.

Salt is important; I read that somewhere – not that I'm going to do a real spell or anything. I wouldn't know how but if when I'm really concentrating, all alone in the middle of the wood, if then Peter does come back I don't want any old evil spirit sneaking along with him and evil spirits don't like salt. That's why you should always throw a pinch of salt over your left shoulder if you spill any, to get the devil in the eye.

Now.

I close my eyes and start. I'm slap in the middle of

the clearing in the only spot where the sun shines through. It is warm on my face. I try to conjure up a picture of Peter but it's hard, other pictures keep getting in the way. I wish I'd brought the photograph.

Concentrate.

I do. I stand very still. I stand like that for ages. The backs of my legs begin to itch and I feel hot and slightly giddy. Is this the right time for a spell? Shouldn't it be at night with a full moon? I don't know but I won't give up.

And then very slowly something begins to happen. I hear noises, as if the wood is breathing and shuffling very quietly towards me. I keep my eyes tightly shut and my fists clenched.

It's him, I know it is. I'm not making it up, really I'm not. I can sort of see him, as if he is far off. I can't see his face properly; it's like he's on the far side of a road. He has his hand up. Perhaps he's waving. I wish he would come a little closer.

He does.

I hear steps, very soft. Then silence.

'It's all right.' The words just come out as a breath, hardly that. Not enough to frighten him away: not enough to spoil the moment.

'What you on about?'

Oh no! This is terrible. It's not him! It's not Peter. That wasn't his voice at all. It's not fair, I wasn't conjuring and now what have I got – a demon? It can happen, I know, I've read about it happening, but I don't know what you're meant to do. I can feel a major panic attack beginning. I may look calm most of the time but that's just a disguise – underneath there's panic. I have to stay inside the circle. I know that much. How do you make demons go away? 'Go away!'

'Wha'?' The voice sounds puzzled but that doesn't fool me.

'Go away! Go back where you came from.' And then: 'Shoo!'

'You wha'?'

That doesn't sound like a demon. They can be tricky though and disguise themselves. I'm keeping my eyes shut because if it's what I think it is, it can't do anything to me unless I look at it.

'Why you breathin' funny?'

I'm not breathing funny: I'm breathing like a train and I want to scream. I can feel one building up. I want to scream because I'm panicking and I'm so stupid.

'Wha' you doin' standin' there like that?'

'Go away.'

'Are you daft or something?'

'No, I'm not.'

'You don' half look it.'

'I don't.'

'How do you know wha' you look like: your eyes are all squinty up.'

'Bet you don't look any better. You've probably

24

got horns, and a black tongue and a nose like a pig and –'

'Nose like a pig!' There are a few experimental grunts. 'I think I do!' There's more grunting and snuffling, right up to the edge of my circle and I don't mean to but I look.

It's the boy Mum nearly ran into when we arrived. I wish she had. I plomp down in the middle of my circle. I feel like shouting at him, but he looks quite funny with his nose in the dirt and his bottom in the air. And I want a pee.

He snuffles over to a mossy stump and then sits down. 'What you doin'?'

'Spell.' I wish I really could cast one on him.

'Wha'?'

'Spell.' He's probably a bit thick.

'Is that what you're bein', a witch?'

'It's not a game.'

'That right?' Something catches his attention on the ground by his feet. He reaches down and a spider runs on to his hand. I hate spiders; they're disgusting. He studies it for a moment, then lets it go again. 'I don't believe none of that stuff – witches 'n' that.'

I shut my eyes, hoping he'll go away.

'Aren't you goin' to carry on then?'

I feel like stamping my foot but you can't do that when you're sitting cross-legged on the ground and want a pee.

How can I carry on with him there asking stupid

questions? 'It's not just ordinary magic you know.'

'That right?'

I don't want to explain about Peter and everything; he wouldn't understand anyway. I decide he needs frightening and I know just what I can tell him but I can't remember the word; it's for a dangerous spell, that's what I read. And then I have it. 'I was doing a summoning. Do you know what that is?' I can sound just as snooty as Mum sometimes.

'I know what a summons is. Leastways my brother does.'

'Is it to do with bringing back someone who's dead?'

'Don't be daft.'

I ignore that. 'Everything has to be exactly right for a summoning and if there's an interruption it can be mortally dangerous.'

'Mortally?' He says it like he's trying it out. I knew that would stump him.

'But you don't believe in any of it do you?'

'What's so dangerous 'bout it then?'

A challenge. I can hardly ignore that can I? 'All right,' I say, 'I'll tell you, if you really want to know.' And I tell him a story about my Aunt Hilda (except I don't have an Aunt Hilda) who is the grand witch of a coven, and extremely powerful but, unusually for a witch, she loves animals, always rescuing strays and finding them homes. He is listening closely now. So I make the story all about a dog she found and

26

loved and cared for. But the dog got run over and she was so upset she tried to bring it back in a summoning but she was interrupted by the children who lived next door, right at a crucial moment, and it distracted her, of course, and the dog, Joe, that was his name, came back, but when she saw it she wished she had left it in peace . . .

'Why?'

Now I'm actually not sure what to do to the dog in the story. I don't really like dogs anymore but the boy does obviously. 'He came back,' I say stalling a little bit, 'and looked perfect, but when he jumped up to lick my aunt, she saw that he had no tongue.'

'No!'

'He had something wrong with his throat too; it was all twisted in a knot and he couldn't swallow his food.'

'Did he die then?'

'You can't die twice, didn't you know that?' He shakes his head. 'But he starved and as his body grew more and more thin, his eyes grew bigger and bigger, so that they looked like great pale, blood-rimmed lamps. She couldn't keep him of course. You can't when something like that happens.'

He nods as if he knows this only too well. I almost believe it myself; it's a funny thing but when I'm making things up, sometimes I do sort of believe me.

'So what happened to Joe?'

'Became a night dog – half dead, half living. Disappeared into the hills. She could hear it howling sometimes and sometimes a thin shadow would move across her garden to her, and she would know it was her dog because of this unbearable feeling of sadness and hunger. But there would be nothing she could do except talk gently to it, and eventually the shadow would glide away.'

He kind of shakes himself, a bit like a dog really, and looks embarrassed. 'You're 'aving me on, ain't you?'

Of course I am, but he sounds almost respectful. I knew he was stupid. 'Slit my throat and hope to die.'

'You really can do spells then?'

'I'm only learning.'

'But nothing happened just now, did it?'

'I don't know.' I'm telling the truth now. I had sort of brought Peter back, hadn't I? I wasn't making that up. 'You don't always know straight off. I might have conjured something up that's in the wood right now.' It *is* possible. I remember that feeling I had of the wood breathing and moving, and it was before the boy sneaked up, I'm sure of it. The day seems to have become cooler, and I shiver.

Suddenly he scrambles up one of the trees and hangs upside down from a branch. 'I gave you a fright, din' I?'

'No.'

He's like a bat the way he hangs; his huge T-shirt

bagging down leaving his tummy bare. He's very skinny, and he has these large, believing eyes.

'You got a funny smile,' he says. 'D'you know that?'

I shrug and stop smiling, but he doesn't seem to notice. 'When you were standing with yer eyes shut. You din' hear me did you?'

'No, but I was concentrating, you see when . . .'

I'm quite impressed with the way he can hang like that swinging backwards and forwards, just hanging on with the crook of his knees, but I don't think he's very interested in my magic anymore which surprises me.

'What's your dad do?' he asks.

'Airline pilot.' I want to get home before it gets late and Mum sends Uncle John out to look for me. She'd skin me if I was found here.

'Pilot, not bad that. Mine's got a garage back in the village. He could fix that old car of yours easy. He's a top mechanic, my dad . . .'cept, he's not that well a lot of the time. I can fix things too.' He reaches up, grips the branch, unhooks his legs and swings down, all in one easy movement like they do it in the circus. He walks up to me. I stand up. 'I know all about the wood,' he says. 'Anything you want to know, I can tell you.' He cocks his head. 'Well?'

'Well what?'

'Anything you want to know?'

'Not really.' I don't mean to be unfriendly. I just

can't think of anything. He looks disappointed and then, quite suddenly, his face changes. I've never seen anything like it; it goes stiff and white, even with all his freckles. 'Are you all right?'

His voice is barely a whisper. 'I seen one.' His eyes are fixed on something just behind my right shoulder.

I look and don't see anything. He's having me on and I nearly believed him too. I'm impressed; I don't usually fall for stories and things like that because it's *my* speciality, telling big ones – that's what Mum calls it. She hates me making things up. 'What was it?' I let him carry on.

Then I notice he's not beside me anymore but backing away very cautiously as if he doesn't want to frighten a shy animal.

'There.'

This time I see what he's seen and I get such a fright it's like someone has punched me on the heart.

'Come on!'

I'd only read about them in books, in stories. Didn't even believe in them, not really. And now I can't move and it's all my fault because a face bunched round with wild, grey hair is staring through the bushes with greedy eyes, as if she wanted to eat us up – like witches do.

CHAPTER FOUR

'Good morning class.'

The room is bright with posters and drawings; the tables are grouped in pairs so that the children work facing each other, like in my London school. A large window looks out on to the school yard and the sun is shining. It's Monday and despite all my very best arguments, I'm here doing my best not to scowl.

'Can't see why you should fuss,' Mum said. 'It's my first day too.' She means her new job in Uncle John's estate office in the village – secretary. I don't think she'll be much good somehow. Just a feeling.

'Morning, Miss Tracy.'

Miss Tracy has yellow hair, a pale face and bright red lips. She's wearing a yellow jumper and baggy blue trousers. I think she looks nice; cheerful like the room. Not like her, the one in the wood. I had dreams last night.

'Sit down everyone.'

Everyone sits except me. I'm standing beside Miss Tracy and she's holding my hand. If she weren't hanging on to me I'd be out of here like a singed rat. It doesn't matter what grown-ups say, things don't get easier the taller you get.

All the children are wearing white shirts and ties, and they all have clean scrubbed faces. They're all looking at me. I could kill Mum because she said there wasn't a school uniform and I knew there would be, and then when we found out, it was too late to do anything. 'You know I'm not good at details, Kate.' That is what she said. Terrific.

'This is Katherine Gaveston. She's just moved to Bexstead from London.' Her voice has a soft burr but her hand is surprisingly hard. 'We must all do our best to make her feel at home, mustn't we?' Miss Tracy smiles at me. It's a lovely smile and she is probably the nicest teacher I'm likely to have; but even good teachers do the wrong thing most of the time.

A couple of girls sitting up near the front smile at me encouragingly. They want me to be interesting and unusual, all of them do. I want me to be interesting too but there's no chance of that happening suddenly. If you try to be funny, you're a show off; if you don't you're boring. And if I told them that I wanted to be a witch, though not one like her in the woods, they'd say it was stupid. On your first day at school the children in your class actually want you to be something like a Martian; or a ballet-dancing princess who comes to school in a Rolls Royce; or a freak who can walk on the ceiling. After a couple of weeks, though, they'd probably start picking on you for being different.

'She can sit with us, miss,' says one of the encouraging girls.

'That's kind of you, Helen.' This niceness is getting a bit much. Helen has soft eyes, and a mulberry coloured stain on her cheek – a birth mark I suppose, or she walked into a lamp-post on the way to school. It's lucky about the mark because the girl sitting next to her has the same kind of soft eyes and stuff like that, and I wouldn't be able to tell one from the other. But I give her a grateful look and make to go towards her, but miss has still got a tight grip on my hand.

'Before you sit down, Katherine,' she says, 'would you like to tell the class a little bit about yourself?'

I certainly would not.

'Katherine?'

I manage at last to blather out some nonsense before lockjaw sets in. And do you know what I say? I say I believe in ghosts, because I do (not that I really think that Peter is a ghost, he's just Peter). That was OK, no one minds that sort of thing too much, but when I get stuck and say I believe in ballet I can see thirty pairs of eyeballs bulging at me. What do I mean 'believe in ballet'? Pure panic. I hate ballet anyway. Fortunately before Miss Tracy can do anything more than look a bit surprised, there's a major diversion.

The class door swings open and there's the boy from the woods. Talk about ghosts! It's like he's haunting me, except ghosts don't run away, and he did from the witch woman. I've never seen anyone move like that. I lost sight of him in about half a minute and then I had to find my way out on my own. I wouldn't have minded only she was following me, I was sure of it. I heard her calling.

Uncle John had gone when I got back but Mum was in such a good mood she didn't even ask where I'd been, or notice the scratches on my legs. She was busy clearing out the garage so she can paint in there.

'Morning, miss.'

The boy doesn't seem to see me. He's not in school uniform and he looks like an imp: small and skinny with a streak of oily black on his cheek and a fake sorry expression on his face.

'Why are you late, James?'

'Traffic jam in the high street, miss. Honest.' Some of the children giggle and I get the feeling this is a regular performance. 'You really wouldn't believe –'

'No, Jimmy, I wouldn't.' Miss sounds bored. 'I warned you last week so off you go to Mr Wootton. You can tell *him* about the traffic in Bexstead. I don't want to hear about it anymore.' Most of those who'd been laughing stop now and look uncomfortable. One or two look smug; I notice that one of them is Helen.

I saw Mr Wootton on my way into the school. He is the head, and the sort of person you can have nightmares about – sideburns that tuck under his chin, nose like a spike and coconut hair that brushes the wrong way across his head.

'Please, miss.' Jimmy is looking uncomfortable too.

'I brought you an owl pellet I found down in the woods. I think there's a barn owl there, miss, and you were talking about them . . .' He is holding out a little brown furry thing; it looks pretty disgusting to me.

Miss Tracy takes it and puts it on her desk. 'Thank you,' she says. 'Now off you go.'

I think that's mean. If someone gave me a present I wouldn't send them off to the headmaster even if it did look disgusting.

'Serves 'im right, the silly berk.' Someone at the back says this, one of the boys. If Miss Tracy hears she ignores it. Jimmy shrugs unhappily and goes out.

I join Helen's table and the morning begins. The class is doing project work on the village. My last school was always doing projects, mainly about Victorians and children slaving away down in coal pits. This is local history and it's quite interesting because there's discussion about Uncle John's building site and the little estate where we live. I don't say anything because most of the class don't like the idea of lots of new houses but apparently Uncle John has agreed to let the school come out to the site in the woods later this week. I bet he ends up convincing the whole village that his buildings are just what they want. Mum says he's a clever man.

Playtime comes and there's still no sign of Jimmy, not that I care. He's probably run off. I sit down on the little wall at the edge of the play area.

'Is your uncle really married to a princess then?'
It's Helen and a few of the others clustered around.

'Mm.'

'I told you, didn't I?' she says triumphantly to the
others. 'And your dad, what about him?'

'Cancer.'

They're impressed. 'Is he dying then?' she asks
softly.

I look down at my hands folded on my lap. I am
quite upset at the thought of Dad only having six
months to live; even if it's not true. 'Yes.'

There's a murmur of sympathy. 'Would you like
us to leave you on your own?' This is Janet, the one
without the mulberry mark. I nod.

'Is he a baldy?'

A fat boy asks this. One of the girls jabs him but
he's not put off. 'From the kimertherapy, you know.
Is he?'

I wonder whether to answer. I don't know what
kimertherapy is.

'My auntie lost all her hair. Right shiny on top
now. Is your dad like that?'

'Oh shut up, Simon! No one's interested in your
duffy old aunt.'

But even though he's jabbed and shoved he hangs
on, so finally I say, 'Some people lose their hair: my
father hasn't.' I sound pretty snooty if you ask me
but I've begun to enjoy myself. It always happens if
I let myself get carried away: Dad a dying musician,

36

uncle married to an African princess and living with a tribe of pygmies (I think Peter would like that); Mum and me living on our own together because Mum has had a row with the rest of her family (who are wealthy, of course) and they've disowned her . . . And then I see Jimmy standing at the back of the little group. My stories trail off and then the bell goes. Helen puts her arm through mine as we walk back to the classroom.

It always happens, but I still hate it when people find out that I make up things a little. I rather wish Jimmy hadn't turned up then, and that fat boy, Simon, keeps staring at me and then he goes up to miss, I knew he would. Jimmy sits with the noisy boys and is sent out twice but Miss Tracy never shouts at him, and he's never rude to her. I'm glad of that.

When the bell goes at the end of the day, Miss Tracy keeps me behind and while she tidies up her things, stacking up little exercise books and sliding them into a plastic shopping bag, she asks me how the day was, and all that and then she says, 'Can I tell you a secret?'

'Of course, miss.' I love secrets.

'My sister died of cancer last year.'

I concentrate grimly on her shoes. The funny thing is that it's her smell I notice. Roses, I think.

'It's not the sort of thing I tell people normally. And it's not really the way to make friends either, telling stories like that, is it?'

As it happens I know more about how not to make friends than anyone else in the universe, but I don't think this is the time to tell her.

'Do you make up stories quite a lot?'

A bee has blundered into the classroom and keeps banging against the window.

'A bit.'

She smiles suddenly. 'Perhaps you should write a book?'

'You won't tell my mum?'

'Not this time, but watch yourself, Katherine, all right?'

I certainly shall. I shall watch myself like a hawk.

Of course I don't and when I come tearing round the corner towards the library I run smack into Mr Wootton. Bam! Like running into a rock, except this one has got grippers – he grips my shoulder. He does not smell of roses. 'I'm terribly sorry.' If I had a penny every time I said that I'd be a millionaire and wouldn't have to go to any school at all. He doesn't say anything, just holds me there for a minute, and then lets me go. Probably doesn't know who I am.

I practically creep through the lobby and then, once outside, fly across the playground and out through the gates. Freedom.

'Watcha.'

Jimmy's squatting down, his back against the pillar.

'Hi.'

'You don't call yourself Geoffrey in school, do you?'

'No.'

He jumps up and walks beside me. He's got a sort of bouncing walk, all up on his toes. I suspect it's from running away so much. I'm not sure I want him walking along with me. I bet he's going to have a go, like Miss Tracy did. Anyway he's a bit smaller than I am and so skinny his T-shirt looks like it's about to flop off. 'Why don't you wear a shirt and tie?' Perhaps if he doesn't have to wear a uniform I won't either and that wouldn't be bad.

'Miss give you a telling off?'

'Sort of.'

'In trouble?'

'No.'

'Really? I'm always in trouble. Bet you talked yourself out of it, right? I wish I could do that. Tell a load of zippers did you?'

I don't know what he's talking about.

'Zippers. Wallops . . .' He looks at me as if I came from another planet. 'Lies, you know.'

I know. 'No, I didn't.'

'Just to the others, then?'

I shrug a sort of yes. I don't like him thinking I tell lies all the time. 'Only part of what I told you wasn't true.'

'I know that. That woman came right out of the wood, after all your magicking, didn't she? I didn't

39

mean to leave you behind. I sort of forgot you wouldn't know your way so quick like.'

'Why did you pretend in school that you hadn't seen me before?'

'Miss would've been upset if she thought we were mates.'

Is that what we are?

Suddenly he grabs my arm and darts across the road and barges through the door of a little, old sweet shop. 'This is where I work – do my rounds.' A bell tinkles as we go in.

Behind the counter is an elderly lady with a whiskery chin. She's little too. I think everything in Bexstead is little and old. She smiles. 'Hello dear, is this a friend of yours? The new family that's come, are you?' She sounds nice.

'Can we have some sweets, Miss Green?' says Jimmy, loudly.

'In them new houses, is that where you're staying?'

'Yes.'

'Sweets, Miss Green,' says Jimmy again. She might be a little deaf as well as just little. He points to the jars on the top shelf, and when she turns to reach up, he winks at me and pinches two bars of chocolate from the counter.

I hate that sort of thing. It's mean. And stupid. 'Put them back.'

'What?'

'Back.' I give him a sharp nudge.

'Why?'

'Don't you want them, my dear?'

Jimmy hesitates, then says, 'No, sorry, Miss Green, we'll just take a couple of bars. That all right?'

There's a deal of puffing and blowing as she puts the sweets back. 'Course it's all right, my pet. That'll be fifty pence.'

Jimmy fumbles in his jeans pocket but doesn't seem to have any money, so I pay. Outside I push the bars at him and head for home.

'What's up? I'll pay you back.' He has to jog to catch me up.

I tell him what I think about people who go around pinching from little old ladies.

'Her brother don't half exploit me,' he blusters, acting all outraged. I'd like to know where he got a word like exploit from. 'Pays me next to nothing for doing his rounds.'

I walk on without bothering to answer. I'm at the corner before I hear him running after me. 'All right,' he says, giving me the smile he gave Mum the other day, but I'm not falling for it. 'All right, I won't do no more pinching.'

I turn. 'That's up to you.'

'Oh come on, Geoffrey! I thought we could look for that witch, the two of us. That's why I was waiting for you. And I'll show you the wood too. I know it all. I do – badger sets, all kinds of stuff . . .'

I pretend to think it over. 'OK.' And then I've no

idea why, but I say, 'I wouldn't have minded you saying hello in class.'

'Oh.'

He's about as surprised as I am.

It's a stupid thing to say, at least it comes out sounding stupid. I run off.

'I'll come and get you,' he shouts after me. 'In a bit, all right?'

I wave to show I've heard him and then head down the lane that leads from the green to our edge of the village.

CHAPTER FIVE

I pass the church with its dark green and shady grave-yard round it. Graves don't frighten me. In fact I like them, which some people might think weird, but I never think of them as bones and skulls with grinning teeth; I don't know why. Perhaps it's all the names and messages on the stone that I like: 'In loving memory', 'Rest in peace'.

At the corner of the lane I turn right and then, for no reason at all, start to run. I run all the rest of the way back to the estate and then walk slowly past all the new empty houses looking so white and cool and lonely in the afternoon heat. A speckled thrush sits on a fence post and cocks its head at me as I go by, probably wondering why a human has a face like a boiled tomato.

It's so quiet, quieter than the churchyard even. Will no one else move into one of these houses?

Huge excitement – human life spotted! There's a man in blue overalls patching the broken glass in the front door of the neighbouring house. I give him a wave.

He doesn't see me.

On our front doorstep is a large bunch of

carnations, wrapped in cellophane with a pink card tucked into the corner.

Megs.

That's all that's written on the card but I know it's from Uncle John. Stuck to the door is another note, scrawled in purple crayon: *Katie, I won't be long. Key in usual place. Mum.*

It doesn't bother me, her not being here to greet me, even though this was my first day at school. I don't know what she means by 'the usual place'. We haven't been here long enough to have a usual place. I don't feel like going into our empty house anyway, so I just sit and wait for her to come back.

The grass is thin and bone dry, and the earth is prickly hard and crumbles like dust in my fingers. It really is hot but already the shadow from the wood has begun to reach out across the garden. It makes me wonder what it would be like to live right inside a wood. You'd see nothing but trees, and everything would be sort of up and down, not like bars really but like doors, endless doors, and sometimes the doors would open, and then what would you see?

An old face with greedy eyes ... *All the better to see you with.* And perhaps sharp teeth ... *All the better to eat you with.*

Peter would never have run away: he would have gone right up to that old witch and asked her for a ride on her broom. I bet he would have. And she would have said, 'OK', because nobody ever refused

Peter. Bet I'd be different if he was still alive. 'Give us a ride on that broom, then.' Probably wouldn't even say please.

I'm sitting here thinking about all this, quite happy, and watching a daft ant trying to carry a crumb – except to the ant it can't have been a crumb, more like a loaf of bread the size of a piano. Can you imagine going out to do your shopping and coming away from the supermarket with a loaf of bread the size of a grand piano? Anyway this is what I am doing, just daydreaming, when I hear the sound of a bike bell and Jimmy calling.

'Hey, Geoffrey, what you doin'?'

'Waiting for Mum.'

'She not in then?'

I tell him he has a brain the size of a weasel's whisker.

He squats down beside me. 'You know that old woman? I reckon I might know where she lives.' He looks at me like he expects me to say how clever he is, or something like that. I don't. 'Will we go now?'

I shrug. I don't like to think of her, not that I can say that to him. The trees are so close. Is she watching from the shadows?

'Scared?'

What a nerve! I get up and walk straight off towards the path into the wood. What does he know about anything?

He has to jog to catch up. 'Come on Geoff. I just

45

wanted you to come out so as I could show you the gypsy camp.'

There isn't quite room for us to walk abreast so he has to keep ducking back. There's no point in staying angry. The whole thing about being frightened is a bit silly anyway. Everyone gets scared and when you are there's no point in pretending otherwise. You don't have control. At least I don't ... but I don't get frightened that often. And anyhow I wonder what gypsies really look like. There has to be something strange about them else why did Uncle John want to be rid of them. Yes, that must be what the old woman is, and I have to say it makes me feel better, her just being a gypsy not a witch. '*My mother said I never should play with the gypsies in the wood ...*' I never can remember what comes after that.

I let him pass me by and he then leads the way past the clearing and on, deeper and deeper, so that the trees seem to press in around us like a silent crowd. It's so quiet. Just once or twice the wood opens up. We pass a high, sandy bank bathed in sun, a single tree tilts over the top like an old man peering down, and about two thirds up the side of the bank is a round hole like a blind eye. A badger sett he says that is. And further still is a burnt out oak tree, caught by lightning. It reminds me of a giant coffee pot with a stubby, blackened spout. An owl lives there. Jimmy even makes me stop and sniff the air at the foot of the tree. Thick, musky. Fox.

I like that.

I didn't think he would know so much but he does. He spends most of his time here. Old Wood, that's its name. It feels old too; everything staying the same, dying and growing and getting more tangled maybe, but really staying the same. Except for us – people – pinching in from the outside with our little estate. I feel like an intruder.

We cross a stream on stepping stones. It's like something out of one of my books – all overhung with trees, with the water rushing and bubbling by, and there are nine wide, flat, slippery stones right the way across that have been there for ever. And if you look upstream, which I did when I managed to get across, you can see to a place where the stream sort of waterfalls into the pool from high rocks. Jimmy says it's called The Forge. I want to go and investigate but he says he'll take me there another time. He isn't keen on swimming there but he won't say why. Probably not very good. I'm good.

I hadn't realized that it's this stream that runs past the mill; the one that Uncle John wants to make into a fancy house. I don't say anything about this to Jimmy but it's right then when I'm crossing the stream on those slimy stones that I begin to realize just how much Uncle John is going to spoil. Nothing will stop him either; he's one of those people who always gets what they want. I remembered Dad saying that about him ages ago, in one of his early rows with Mum, when he didn't seem to be going into work every day.

Of course I slip off the last stone and dunk my foot in the water. He doesn't laugh which goes to show that though boys are mostly stupid all the time, sometimes they aren't. That surprises me a bit.

He doesn't wait for me, of course, so I have to squelch along behind, until he suddenly motions me to be quiet. He steps off the little track and begins to creep forward on his hands and knees. I follow and I don't complain though I wish I'd changed out of my school clothes. Mum is going to kill me. I mean she'll kill me anyway for mitching off but she'll kill me double if I get all my clothes wrecked.

Anyway I don't really see why we have to do all this sneaking about because of the gypsies, especially since he said he knew them.

'Because we're spyin', aren't we?'

'I've got prickles in my hand.'

'You don't *have* to come.'

Of course I do and eventually we worm our way to the edge of the wood, and there's the camp that we saw yesterday with Uncle John.

There's a gang of kids about our age, chasing about and scrambling over a dump of tyres and chairs and things like that. I can't figure out what the game is, but it's noisy. There's thumping music coming from one of the caravans: *boocha, boocha*. A little baby

48

with no knickers is stamping her foot and shaking her fists in time to the beat which I think is pretty clever but nobody takes any notice of her.

'You really know them?'

'Yeah, course. Said I did, didn' I?'

A small stout woman comes out of the door of a white caravan, bangs a pot with a spoon and yells for the children to come in. For their tea, I suppose. It reminds me that I am hungry. One of the older girls picks up the baby and carries her in.

To the right is a scrap of a field with a shaggy looking pony grazing in it; beyond that is the road and on the far side I can just make out the tall wire fence of Uncle John's site.

At that moment a motorbike bumps off the road and down the far side of the paddock, disappearing behind the caravans. It's then I notice the old house, a cottage it is really, about a hundred yards beyond the furthest caravan, tucked up against the edge of the wood, the green of the trees seeming to reach almost right round it. The roof has a deep sag as though a giant has sat on it, and the chimney's lopsided. Broken windows stare towards the camp.

'Used to be the wood keeper's,' Jimmy says when I ask him. 'My dad said there was a murder done there. The last keeper.'

A murder! Yes, it looks just the sort of place.

Then I see her. 'Look!' I'm sure it's her, walking

away from the caravans towards the cottage. Without thinking I stand up to try to get a clearer view of her, but she has her head down and Jimmy grabs my leg to pull me out of sight and I kick him because he's accidentally pinched me. Some spies!

'What you up to?' A gypsy with a black beard covering half his face and sleeves rolled back to show off his black hairy arms, is standing on the steps of the nearest caravan staring straight at me. 'Get out of there, you kids,' he shouts, immediately jumping down the steps and starting towards us.

'Tell them who you are,' I hiss.

'Don't be stupid.' Jimmy is already wriggling back into the undergrowth. 'Geoff, come on.'

I can't move. It's the story of my life. I'm not frightened, just sort of stuck. It must be pretty annoying to have to rely on someone like me, I think.

'Geoff!'

Rabbits get hypnotised don't they? Hypnotised and then bitten by the fox, but no fox would ever get me. I would stare it out. Behind the gypsy I notice a group of men who've drifted round the corner of the caravans. There seems to be a fair bit of arm waving and angry voices though I don't think it's anything to do with me. Two of them break away. One of them is the motorcyclist. 'What's up, Jacko?'

The dark gypsy has a big belly and a rolling walk and the sun glints on a ring in his ear. A gold earring! He's just like he's meant to be. Then he stops. We're close enough to spit at each other. 'Kids,' he shouts over his shoulder. I can see the sweat patches under his arms. 'Some spying little kids.'

I narrow my eyes and stare at him so hard I can almost see right through him. Then he sort of shakes himself the way a dog does when it's been irritated by a fly.

'Geoff, please.' Jimmy's voice sticks to me like a pin. I take a step backwards though I know Jacko would never touch me. I feel like there's a barrier right there and he can't cross it.

'Clear off,' he growls. 'Next time I'll set me dogs on you.' He suddenly turns and walks towards the others. I quickly step back behind a tree and lean up against it. Yes! I'm breathing quickly and my heart bangs like a drum.

'Been seeing things, Jacko?' A different voice, younger. 'Been down to the boozer already?' And a laugh, but cold not friendly.

'I thought there were two of them,' says Jacko. 'But I dunno . . .' Their voices fade. Funny, I didn't think he had seen Jimmy.

'I thought he was going to slaughter you,' hissed Jimmy.

'Maybe I put a spell on him. What do you think?'

'You're cracked.' He turns away and takes the lead back. I follow behind. Of course he acts like it wasn't a big deal but, when we reach the stream and we've stopped and sloshed water on our faces and we've talked about the old woman, our witch, and have decided that she must be one of the gypsies, right out of the blue he says, 'If them others had seen me, they'd have killed us. Killed me anyway.'

'I thought you said you got on OK with them.'

He flicks a stone into the stream. 'Because the one who came on the bike, with the leathers, you know, that walked over, yeah, well, that's my brother. I didn't know he was hanging round with that lot. Bad sticks to bad.'

'Like you and me?' I say.

'Mebbe.' He smiles, but a bit sadly it seems to me. Weird to have a brother and not like him.

'Would your brother have let them hurt you?' Even as I asked the question I remembered his voice – cold and thin as a needle.

'Would he what? Frank! Be the first to put the boot in, and think it a joke.'

Neither of us feel like chatting after that. I have too much on my mind; too many questions and too many worries. Why is Jimmy's brother so horrid to him? Why is she right over on our side of the wood, ready to eat us up, if she's just an old gypsy woman? Why didn't that fat gypsy chase us? Had I frightened him? I didn't think so, not really, but you never know. And what will I say to Mum? That's why it takes me by surprise when, just as we are coming out of our side of the wood, and my house is up in front of us, he says, 'Is your mum nice?' It isn't even like she's standing at the gate waiting, thank goodness, but it startles me all the same. I hate it when someone cuts in on your thoughts, like they've been peeking about in your mind. 'Why?'

'Just wondered.' He picks up his bike. 'See you tomorrow, OK?' And he's off.

Is Mum nice? I've never thought about her like that. She's just her: moody, jumpy, pretty ... My bag has gone from the path, and so have all the carnations. They've been stuffed round the house by now. Sugar and spice and all things nice – what are mothers made of? I brush my skirt down. It isn't too bad. Then I wander into the garage and see that she has cleared a space by her easel. It's about time she began painting again.

CHAPTER SIX

I think my head's like the inside of our laundry basket, it's so tumbled up and messy, and I don't know what's what anymore.

Jimmy came into school, late as usual, said 'How 'ya?', quite friendly and all that, and then he went to sit over with the boys at the back.

I don't give tuppence – Mum always says that when she doesn't care about something. Anyway, I prefer being on my own. The others are stupid. Simon, the fat one, keeps turning around and sticking his tongue out at me and whispering out loud how Kate lied. As it happens, I've given up telling stories. What I said yesterday about the gypsies and the one with the earring coming to get me, that was absolute truth. And seeing the old woman over by that house, that was true too. Do you get spots on your tongue from telling the truth the whole time? You do from telling lies; tiny pimples.

What I didn't tell you was what happened when I got home yesterday after being at the gypsy camp. Mum was there, of course, in the kitchen with a face that would deep freeze a week's supply of chicken legs, and all those pink and white carnations that had been left on the front door step stuffed around the place, as I knew they would be. And then there was Mum sitting at the table, grinding half a cigarette into a saucer.

'Where have you been?' It wasn't a great start.

I tried to be friendly. 'Nice flowers, Mum.'

She glared at me and quite suddenly I knew she didn't like them either. 'Where?' she repeated.

Tactic number two – invent. I told her that I had been on a cycle ride on my bike and I went on about how brilliant the bike was, because I thought that might please her. It didn't. I'd forgotten I'd left the bike behind when I'd gone off into the wood. Rapid invention. 'Well, you see after the ride, I walked out to the Mill House, the one Uncle John showed us, you remember . . .' She wasn't looking any more friendly '. . . and played by the stream there.'

'You weren't in the wood.'

'The wood? No.'

Inventions to get out of trouble are not the same as stories.

I think she partly believed me. She sounded a little less inhuman when she said she didn't like me going off on my own. I really have to remember that when I try to make compliments and be extra nice to her, she gets angrier. 'I went with that boy from school. He's really friendly. You know, the one you nearly knocked off his bike . . .'

'That was his fault.' She lit up another cigarette and put the kettle on. Good sign.

I told you she was mad about me making friends, so I rubbed it in. 'Actually we're quite good friends . . .' I studied the card that had come with the flowers, pretending to be casual, but half watching her just to see how she reacted to this. I can be quite devious sometimes. At the very least she hadn't said anything about my one squelchy foot, or the grass stains on my school skirt. Why didn't I at least leave my shoes outside? You see I have to be devious because otherwise I would be in perpetual, one hundred per cent, ultimate trouble.

'Oh,' she said, 'what's his name?'

'Jimmy.'

'Would you like a cup of tea?'

'Please.' You see. Plain sailing when you know how. 'Uncle John doesn't usually send flowers does he?' She gave me one of those *what did you mean by that* sort of looks. I'm only making conversation, or trying to. I sat down and stretched out my legs and, in a manner of speaking, put my great big foot right in it, because she immediately saw that my shoes were soaking wet.

'Those were brand new shoes.' Eyes like razors. Then, of course, she noticed the stains on my dress. 'You did exactly what I told you not to do, didn't you?' She was very cross. She didn't shout but spoke in a way that I hate; so I feel like a baby, irresponsible,

56

as if I can't look after anything or be trusted. 'You'll come straight to the office, every day after school. Do you hear me, Kate? And you can do your homework there.'

I couldn't say anything back to her but I slammed the door and ran up to my room.

It was only when I had cooled down and was looking out over the forbidden wood, Rabbit on the sill beside me (it's become a bit of a habit, that looking out over the wood in the evening before going to bed), that I wondered why she'd looked so miserable with all those flowers she'd been given around her. I thought everybody was supposed to love being given flowers. Perhaps she hates pink as much as I do.

Anyway, you'll be glad to know I dealt with fat Simon. I got a corner of drawing paper soaked in red paint, squeezed tight till it had the texture of a wet stone and then flicked it with unbelievable accuracy from the edge of my table to the tip of his right ear. And before he could even scream, I was walking up to Miss Tracy's desk to ask if I could go to the toilet. Serve him right. He squawked and started blaming everyone around him – except for me of course. Miss Tracy told him to stop fussing. I like her.

The only trouble with sitting on your own is when you have to do group work. I hate that – being glued on to some other table where they don't want you, and you don't want to be there. So my heart sank when Miss Tracy announced the project we were all going to be working on – not the subject, that was all right, we were going to do work on the village, any aspect that we wanted, like the history of the church, or finding out how the mill worked, all that kind of thing – but that she recommended we worked in threes or fours.

Of course everybody else was sitting in threes and fours so they were all right. I ducked, hoping she wouldn't notice me.

Then, to my astonishment, I hear Jimmy speaking up. 'All right if we work in pairs, miss?'

'I suppose so, James,' she says. She sounds a bit doubtful, but I think that's only because she doesn't trust Jimmy one little bit. I'm not sure how much I trust him either. 'Who are you going to work with?'

'Geoff – I mean Kate Gaveston, miss.'

'Oh?' She looks like someone has stamped on her foot. 'With Kate?' I must say I'm a bit offended. It's not like I've got the plague or something. 'Do you want to work with James, Katherine?'

Well that puts the shoe on the other foot, I suppose. I look across at Jimmy. He's gone a bit pink and is standing at his table, trying to ignore the lads who are poking him and giggling. One of them grabs his sleeve and tugs it, trying to get him to sit down. Perhaps they reckon he's making a fool of himself. Perhaps he is.

'Yes,' I say, suddenly finding my voice, and then heaven knows what pops the words on to my tongue, but I add, 'We're going to do a project on the wood.'

Jimmy nods. It's like that was what he had had in mind anyhow. 'Old Wood, miss. We talked about it already, see.'

We hadn't.

'That's a good idea,' she says.

'Yeah, we thought so.' Then he nearly ruins it all by thumping the boy who had been tugging at his sleeve. To my surprise he isn't sent out but told to come away from his own table and, since there isn't really another table for him to go to, he joins me, and that is the way it happens. And he's grinning – I think if boys can hit someone it always makes them feel better – while I'm a bit embarrassed. I don't go bright pink like him though.

'How'd you know I were goin' to say the Old Wood?'

'I dreamed it last night,' I say, looking at my nails.

'That's a load of cobblers.'

'And I dreamed about that old woman too.'

'Did you?'

I did. I dreamed she was in the house, actually in the house. Can you imagine anything more creepy? Out on the landing, watching me, and then, in my dream, I went downstairs and she was under the kitchen table.

We talk about whether she's really a witch or not. Somehow, here in the classroom, it doesn't seem so likely, though the dream did make me wonder a bit because I believe witches can get inside your dreams, that's one of their ways of controlling you. Anyway, we decide she can't be, not really, so she can spy as much as she wants, she won't frighten me.

He's busy scratching away at a drawing with his pencil all the time he's talking, the top of his tongue poking out of his mouth. Then he suddenly stops and looks at me. 'I got an idea for the project.'

'About the wood?'

'Yeah. You know the pool below The Forge? I showed it to you.' He lowers his voice. 'A girl drowned there. Nobody knows how it happened. She was found floating, face down, dead as a mat. We could find out, like do an investigation. It were a long time ago, but it'd be great in our project. What do you think?'

Is he making it up? I'm about to say, 'Listen, I'm the one who tells the stories,' but I don't. He couldn't tell a lie to save his life, not that sort of lie anyway. Dead as a mat. I don't know if I want to swim there now.

'Great.'

'You don't sound too interested.'

Then I tell him how Mum has grounded me and, apart from all this homework routine in the office, I'm not allowed to go anywhere, anywhere at all.

'Are you serious? What about our project?'

'She's mad. I can't help it.'

He frowns and looks back down at his drawing,

and then adds a couple of heavy lines. 'Well, she can't stop us, and I tell you something else, I reckon we should explore that old cottage; the one the old woman come out of. I told you the last keeper was murdered there, my dad said. I can ask him about that and about what the wood were like then; he were always hunting. That'd make two things already for our project. What do you say, Geoff? It'd be the best thing ever, best thing I ever done.'

'We can ask Mum, I suppose.'

'Course we can.' He twists his drawing round so I can see it. It's excellent: a rat with its tail curled up round it.

'Otter,' he says proudly. Then, sounding just like Uncle John, 'All right, I'll see what I can do.' Of course he's just being a big head, but he means to be nice. That's what I presume anyhow. Then to my utter amazement he marches up to Miss Tracy and starts talking to her. At first she shakes her head, and then I can see her taking him more seriously. She looks across at me and then she pulls her pad towards her and starts to write. In a couple of minutes he's back, looking very self-important. 'This'll do for the job,' he says and waves an envelope under my nose. On the outside is written, *Mrs Gaveston*.

'What did she write?'

'You'll find out. We'll deliver it after school, OK?'

I am impressed, though of course I don't show it. Even so, I can't seriously believe Mum will change

61

her mind but we act as if she will and spend the rest of the afternoon talking about what sort of things we will find out for our project: we are going to map the wood and find out its history. Jimmy thinks Mr Vine might help us with that, he's the man ('the squire' he calls him) who lives up in the big house on the hill, the one Uncle John is planning to buy. Also we're going to catalogue, that's my word, all the animals. But the most important section is going to be the mystery of the drowned girl. I am going to do most of the writing; Jimmy can do the drawing. He's so excited by it all that twice he has to get up and run round the classroom and thump one of the boys. Luckily Miss ignores him.

At three-thirty we go out of school together and up to the main street to Mum's office. I try to put him off. I even try to get him to give me the letter and let me do it on my own. I don't want him there, hearing her getting cross with me again. But he's quite cocky, thinking he can persuade her.

CHAPTER SEVEN

Everything's blue and grey in Mum's office, even the men who work there.

There are only two of them and they're both on the phone when we go in. The one called D. Jenks – they both have blue and grey nameplates on their desks – beckons us over. 'Oh no, no, no, madam,' he's saying into the phone, his voice oozing. 'Oh no, no. This is exclusive, I assure you . . .' There's no sign of Mum. She said she'd be here.

Jimmy's flicking through the stacks of glossy brochures – all for Uncle J's properties – ignoring D. Jenks who's waving his hand as if he'd like to swat Jimmy away like a fly. I plump myself down in a chair.

Mr Jenks puts his hand over the phone. 'You're not Margaret's little girl?' I've never heard Mum being called that.

'Yes.'

He looks a bit surprised. 'You'd better go into her office, hadn't you?'

Why do some grown-ups do this sort of thing? Make you wait. Make you stand. It gives me the creeps.

*

Instead of facing on to the street, Mum's office has a window looking out on to a paved yard with a couple of cars parked in it. It's a scorcher of a day. A dog noses in through the gate and flops down in the thin shadow of the side wall and lies there, head up, tongue hanging out. A cream-coloured car pulls up across the gateway. It looks a bit like Uncle John's. At that moment, in walks Mum.

Do you know what her first words to me are? I'll tell you: 'Have you got your homework with you?' Not 'Hello' or 'Is this the boy you were telling me about?' Nothing civilized like that, just 'Have you got your homework with you?' I could have shrivel-led her up and turned her into one of Jimmy's owl pellets.

'No.' Jimmy nudges me in the ribs. 'This is Jimmy, Mum.'

'How do you do, Mrs Gaveston?' And he's off. My jaw practically hits the floor. She can't get a word in edgeways: the project, working together, he even starts talking about our garden, offering to do a bit of work on it for us. 'I helped out the headmaster for a while; his mum was sick and he'd let the garden go a bit. You know what I mean. I made it nice. You can ask him if you like . . .' I don't know whether Mum believes it or not but she is listening, which is a miracle. 'And here's Miss Tracy's note, I almost forgot to give it you.'

'Oh,' says Mum, taking the letter and glancing at

me. 'Why didn't she give it to Kate? Are you in trouble again, Katherine?'

'No.'

'Oh, it's nothing Mrs G.'

Mrs G! Listen to him! I don't know whether I'm impressed or irritated.

'It were me that asked her for the note. I thought you would probably like to have all the details in writing an' all. And since we're a team, Katherine . . .' he stumbles over my name a bit, 'Katherine and me, it didn't matter who carried it. Right?'

She lights a cigarette while scanning the letter, puffing out a dragon-stream of smoke – I hate her yellow fingers – and then she smiles. 'Well . . .' I knew she would agree then . . . and she does. Of course, I'm pleased. I am really. I just didn't know that Jimmy could be such a talker, that's all.

I think the decider is Jimmy offering to have a go at our garden. She can't resist that. Still, there are restrictions, about a million of them to be precise. We aren't to go beyond the halfway mark (that's the stream), which puts the cottage out of bounds. Jimmy nods as if this is only reasonable. And the list goes on: number two is keeping away from anybody, anybody at all, no matter how harmless they might seem, who we see in the wood; no visits to the gypsy camp – that suits me – no staying out after dark, no going off anywhere on the bikes without telling her . . .

And then we are through and free. And we've still half the day ahead of us. It's only four o'clock and the sun is so hot I can feel it through the soles of my school shoes on the pavement. I want to go to the Forge pool; it'll be cool there and we can plan what to do, and he can tell me about the drowning again – the girl in the pool – and the last woodkeeper from the old cottage. If Mum knew how dangerous the wood was she'd have a fit, and I would have to stay locked up for ever.

Needless to say, Jimmy doesn't want to do what I want to do. 'You won't find out anything just by looking at that old pool,' he grumbles. He wants an ice cream and then for me to go to his house, which is a bit of a surprise.

We compromise. I buy the ice cream with the last of my money and he agrees to come to the Forge.

'You going to swim?' he asks.

'Don't know. Are you?'

He shrugs and looks away.

'Can't you swim?' There I go again.

'Course I can. Just don't feel like it, all right?' End of conversation. I could give lessons on how to annoy people without really trying.

Back at my house, I change like I'd promised Mum I would, putting on my swimsuit, just in case, and an old shirt and my scrambling shorts. I like them, they're cool and baggy and about as different as you can get from slithering Lycra bike-shorts which all the girls in London wore. I can see Jimmy out in the garden wandering about down at the wood end.

I take Rabbit out of my school bag. I don't think I'll bring him to school anymore. I don't say anything to him, just prop him up on my desk where he can look out of the window. He looks a bit glum so I take out my picture of Peter too and put that beside him. I don't know why but I feel a bit guilty.

It's paradise. It has to be. I can't believe a place like this can exist, and certainly not close to where I live. It isn't possible. 'Isn't it private?'

'Why?'

'Don't know. Don't lots of people come here?'

'Some. Not often. Most people don't bother with the wood, and if they swim they go to the baths at Hereford. They got chutes and all that there.'

The pool's not big, about the size of my room I suppose, but it looks as deep as for ever, and trees crowd in round the edges shading all but the very middle of it. The stream pours in through smooth rocks, cutting a deep channel into the stone. Down at the bottom end of the pool, where we are standing, there is a shingly bank, and the stream narrows again to twist round the end of this bank before disappearing down through the wood, past our stepping stones.

Jimmy doesn't know why it's called the Forge. I think it's a good name; sounds old somehow.

We climb up on to the rocks; they're flat-topped and warm from the sun. We both immediately sprawl out on the grey stone. I inch to the edge so that I can peer down and watch the water bulge into the pool. That's where it's deepest, right in the middle. That's where she would have been, the girl, but I can't imagine her. She hasn't got a name or a face yet, that's why.

'Have you ever dived from up here?'

He shakes his head.

'I'm going to.'

'Really?' He keeps looking down into the pool and I take off my shirt and shorts. To tell the truth, I feel a bit awkward, and then, I don't know, I just don't care how knobbly my knees are and lower myself into the fast channel. Better than any swimming pool chute; but the water's so cold the air wooshes out of my lungs and I feel like I'm in the tight grip of an icy jaw.

I think he yells, 'You can't do that!' but my hold is slipping on the smooth stone, my back is raw with the cold and even my bum is ice. I can't see the pool, just the stream of water tearing past my feet and then pouring over the edge.

I let go. A split second of bang and slap and I'm suddenly whapped into the pool, rocked by my own splash and then I windmill to the far side and back again. When I catch my breath I stop swimming and float icily, staring up at the ring of the sky. Then slowly I put my hands up, and let my feet drop. Have you ever done this? And slide down under the surface, keeping my eyes open. I can see the rocks, and green branches, blue sky all wobbling in the broken light. Something touches my foot, it's nothing really but it makes me jerk up to the surface again.

'Hey, Geoffrey!' He's dancing around up on the flat tops. He's stripped down to his pants. He looks silly. He's even more skinny and more white than I am, I think. And he's all arms and legs, leaping from one side of the narrow gorge to the other.

If I had a million pounds I would build a hut and live here and never go anywhere else.

'Geoff-er-ey-fe-ry!' he yells, chanting a slice of my name with each leap.

'You're showing off!'

'No – I'm – not.'

Of course he's showing off; but I don't mind because he looks so funny.

He does a couple more leaps and then runs to the edge of the rock, stops, and I can see him screwing his eyes shut, and then he gives a sort of strangled yelp and flings himself out into the middle of the pool. When he bursts up through the surface again, I nearly laugh out loud; I've never seen anyone look so terrified. His arms are thrashing and splashing and for a moment I think he's not going to make it to the edge. He can't swim at all really but he looks so pleased with himself when he does finally clamber out, that I keep my mouth shut for once. He's pinched and shivering and, of course, hasn't got a towel so I lend him mine. Then we climb back up the rocks to get warm.

We're both silent for a bit. I like this about him, that we don't have to talk. Perhaps that's the trick about friendship; that you don't have to talk all the time. Uncle John never stops but I think that's what Mum likes, probably because she and I hardly speak at all. I wonder about the girl, if she had someone. This would be a lonely place, if you didn't have someone to be with.

I try to imagine only ever hearing the sound of the trees and the scufflings of animals. Perhaps paradise is only paradise if you can visit and don't have to stay.

Did she slip? Or did she jump? If she was lonely she might have jumped. I've never thought about being lonely before. Never. It's never bothered me. I told you that.

Jimmy's lying on his back, his freckled face screwed up against the sun, his hands clasped across his ribby chest. The rock is dark with damp round his red hair, like a black halo. 'Who was she?' I ask. 'Don't you have any idea at all?'

'You thinkin' about the dead girl?'

'Mm.'

'Dad said she come from the big house. She were the sister of the squire, Mr Vine. He lives up there all on his own now. Do you know the house I mean, up on the hill?'

'Yes.'

We're quiet again. Then right out of the blue he suddenly starts to ask me about Mum again.

'Does your mum ever get lonely?'

'How should I know?'

'Doesn't she say?'

'No.' I've never thought about it really I suppose. 'Maybe. She used to go out lots when we lived in London, before Dad left. Doesn't see much of anyone anymore. Probably why she gets so fed up with me all the time.'

'Does she? She doesn't look like she would.'

She's always going on about me having no friends, you'd think she would have hundreds herself, but she doesn't. Probably because she gets angry, and because she smokes all the time.

'My dad complains about being on his own,' says Jimmy, 'even though he's got me running all over the shop for him. He never used to complain about nothin'. Used to be good company. Now he don't want to do nothing half the time, except . . .'

'Except what?'

'I wish you could put one of your spells on my brother.'

'What about your mother? You never talk about her, just always go on about mine.'

'Her insides went funny.' He sounds matter-of-fact.

71

'Then she got so skinny they took her into hospital, in an ambulance; and she never came out again.'

I can remember the ambulance when they took Peter away: cold, white, the door open like a fridge. Then them shutting him away. 'I'm sorry.' I know it sounds empty but I don't know what else you say.

He sits up and I sit up too. We are both facing the pool and he's flicking little shaly stones into the water. I can see them sailing out and making the tiniest of splashes. 'What's there to be sorry about?'

We don't talk for a while. He flips a larger stone and it makes a satisfying 'plop'. 'Wouldn't think you could drown in that, would you?' he says.

I think it looks so dark and green you could drown an army one at a time and no one would ever know. I feel cold across my shoulders and up the back of my neck.

'The Vines owned everything round here one time, like it was their village, so Dad told me. One up there now don't have much left though, just the house I reckon, and Hill Wood.'

'And this wood.'

He shrugs. 'Could do. He caught me rabbitin' up round his place once. Threatened me with a shotgun and all. I knew he weren't going to use it.'

'I don't think anyone should kill rabbits.'

'Why's that then? They're good to eat.'

'Of course they're not. That's disgusting.'

72

He gives me a funny look, then hugs his knees. 'I don't go trappin' anymore anyhow.'

I'm not soppy about animals actually. I don't go round 'ooing' at fluffy puppies and calling everything cute. I just like rabbits. I always have done. I think about Rabbit propped up by my bedroom window, and then I imagine old Mr Vine up in his house looking down on the wood. 'What do you think about us going up to Mr Vine's house, ask him questions, you know, like an interview for our project. It would be great. He might know lots about the wood. He might tell us about his sister too.'

I watch the water sliding like green silk over the grey rock, down the channel, ruffling into white and then into the pool. 'Where do you think she was going when she fell in and drowned?'

'Maybe she weren't going anywhere.'

Drifting through the wood. Yes, I can see that. And I can picture her now in the pool, her white clothes floating out from her. White's a lonely colour and looks ghostly in the half-light of evening; and there are flowers braided in her hair, pale, smoky-blue . . . I almost have to give myself a shake. It's all story book. No one is like that in real life. She probably wore jodhpurs and had a fat, stubby nose. People who wear jodhpurs are never going anywhere.

Jimmy suggests she might have been going over to the gypsy camp but I don't think that's likely; not the squire's daughter.

'I tell you what, let's go and explore the wood-keeper's cottage. Dad told me that he were the meanest man alive. Come on, Geoff, let's go now.'

'But we promised Mum.'

'We didn't.'

He's right actually. We didn't exactly promise; we agreed.

I suppose I knew we would never keep to Mum's rules, but we're not doing anything wrong. I don't think we are anyway.

CHAPTER EIGHT

Perhaps I have some Indian blood in me after all, because I am managing this creeping about business with more success this time, and that's even with my hair dripping down my neck and flopping in front of my eyes like an old, wet curtain. I'm going to cut it all off and have it as short as Jimmy's. When I tell him this, he just says that I would look stupid with short hair.

We skirt round the gypsy camp keeping well into the trees, which is hard since there isn't a path to follow. This side of the wood is different. The trees are, I don't know how to describe it, looser, I think, and then the going gets more difficult and we have to push our way through bushes and saplings. I can't see anything apart from the back of Jimmy's head because, of course, he has to go in front; bobbing up and down with his head like a stupid, peeled orange, his hair being so short.

I get fed up not being able to walk in front. Peter and I always used to run ahead of Mum and Dad on our walks, and I would always run that bit faster than Peter (which wasn't too difficult as he only had stumpy legs). I don't know why I like to be out in front but I do, even when I don't know the way, which is most of the time.

And then, after bashing our way through saplings and bramble, we are practically nose to wall with the back of the old cottage. It looks so sad, half-strangled by trees and with that great sag in the roof, exhausted, as if it were on the point of letting itself slide down into the ground.

There can't possibly be anyone living here. There's a crow's nest up at the top of the chimney, I can see all the twigs and bits sticking out, and there's a black hole in the roof right by the base. It makes me think of tooth decay for some reason. I hate dentists. No one has lit a fire here for years.

I can hear a dog barking from over in the gypsy camp, and a radio playing the same tinny pop music we heard before. I think of that old woodkeeper, murdered. It's the right place for murder, or for going mad. Maybe both. 'Did you ask your dad who did it?'

'What?'

'The murder.'

'No. I forgot.'

How can you forget a murder? Perhaps the gypsies know the story. They should, it all being on their doorstep, so to speak. Trouble is if there's anyone we can't ask, it's them. That one with the earring said he would set his dogs on me – bound to be Rottweilers, and they can tear your throat out. And the old woman with the hungry eyes would eat what was left. Perhaps she was the one who murdered the keeper. I don't know why I frighten myself like this.

Jimmy points to a little window to the right of the door. 'We'll try that.'

The old woman had been going straight for the cottage when I saw her.

'Supposing she's inside?'

'Don't be daft. No one's lived there for ages. I told you.'

I swear if he says that to me again I'm going to clout him into next week.

'And if she's a gypsy, she'll be living in one of the caravans, won't she?'

Such a know-all. 'Well, supposing she isn't. You said you knew them all, didn't you? And you don't know her. Explain that.'

'She's visitin'. They travel about you know, don't always stay in the same place,' and without another word he shoves his way over to the window and I follow behind.

'What are you doing?'

I peer over his shoulder but can hardly see anything through the window, it's so dusty and dark inside. The wood round the hinges is soft; he only needs to dig a little bit with his penknife and he has the whole window unhooked and out of there and neatly propped up against the wall. Then, quick as a rat, he hoicks himself up and slips through into the room.

'Like a thief in the night,' I catch myself saying to myself. And then: 'Has he done this before?' I glimpse his pale face grinning back at me before he disappears into the gloom.

The window sill is gritty and damp, and when I lift myself up and poke my head in I can feel the air stale and musty on my face like cobwebs. A spider the size of a boot tromps across my hand. 'Jimmy?' I hiss. No answer.

Supposing she does live here, and she isn't just an old woman. I remember the way she looked at us.

I'm not going through that window. 'Jimmy?'

'Are you coming?' His voice sounds hollow.

I try the back door and, ridiculously, the handle turns smoothly and the door opens silently.

'How did you do that?'

I shrug. 'Some of my spells do work you know.'

'And I'm Arnold Swarzabeggar.' He touches the door hinge and sniffs his finger. 'Been oiled.'

'Someone's living here, then?'

He makes a face, like it doesn't seem possible. 'Do you want to look round?'

Now we're here, we might as well. We go into the front room. The light shafts greyly in through the windows. Across a playground space of broken green we can see the caravans and figures moving around; and I feel like I'm a thief, stepping into someone else's life.

Behind me is the fireplace littered with rubble and

bits of plaster. There's a tin there too – baked beans – the inside brown and sticky, not that old. There's a picture on the wall, I think it's of a man on a horse but mould has eaten most of it away. There is a scrap of linoleum over by the front door, but the floor itself is uncovered, just dirt and stone. In fact, when I scuff my sandals, I can see it is all stone, big flags. Must have been cold in the winter. A set of stairs leads up from the right of the fireplace. The cottage is so tiny you wouldn't think there was an upstairs – maybe a little attic room.

'Nothing at all,' says Jimmy. He has been moving around, picking and poking quickly; almost like he expected to find treasure.

I don't know why; it's the last place I'd expect to find anything, except a ghost perhaps. I don't like the way the stairs turn at the corner there and end in darkness. I'm sure the woodkeeper wasn't a rich man – the walls are so cold and damp. The whole atmosphere isn't just poor, it's mean.

There's a pile of rubbish in one corner: newspapers, cans, a little posy of withered flowers. 'Someone has been here.'

There are other signs: the wooden chair to the left of the fire isn't covered in dust, and the stone floor round the fireplace is clean too, or at least looks like it might have been swept. Why just that bit of the floor?

'A tramp?'

'Maybe.'

'The old woman? I told you she was walking this way.'

'Shall we go?'

'What about up there?'

I've been trying to ignore the way the stairs beckon. 'It's all right,' he says, 'I'll go.' He goes up carefully but swiftly. 'There're two rooms,' he calls.

'Shh.'

'The door's shut on one.' I can hear him banging at it.

'Leave it!' I suddenly don't like being here at all. 'Come on. Let's go, Jimmy, please.' I don't want to be here when she comes back. I'm sure it is her. I don't want to be here at all.

But we're too late.

As Jimmy reappears at the head of the stairs, a dog whines and scratches at the front door and I hear a voice saying, 'What is it, Laddy?'

CHAPTER NINE

Jimmy jerks his head towards the back room and I slip through. At the same instant the front door rasps as it's shoved open and I make the mistake of looking back. As Jimmy is hustling me to get a move on, I see a hand on the door and the dog, a terrier I think, comes bounding straight towards us.

I hate dogs. They all want to eat me.

'Geoff!'

I can't move. The dog is right by me, and even in the half-gloom I can see that its lips are pulled back and that its teeth are yellow and spitty. It's dying for me to turn and run for it so that it can bite. Then it snaps anyway. I didn't do anything. That's dogs for you – when they know you aren't going to hurt them or anything like that, they want to take a pizza-sized chunk out of you, and they do it quick as lightning, because they know they shouldn't. Of course I'm not thinking all this at the time. What I am doing is making an embarrassing high-pitched squealing noise, a bit like pigs are meant to make, and the horrible little terrier that should be off chasing weasels, is hanging on to the baggy leg of my shorts.

In two strides, Jimmy's over the dog. 'No!'

To my amazement the slavering dog instantly lets go, and cocks its head on one side. I can even see its little tail wagging.

'Good dog.'

I still can't move. My heart is hammering and my legs feel wobbly. Oddly, it's the way Jimmy is softly murmuring to the terrier that somehow surprises me. He sounds so different. I can't explain how, it's just different.

I suppose the gypsy had seen everything and probably was disappointed we hadn't both been torn to shreds. 'All right, now maybe you want to explain what you doing 'ere, eh?' he says and snaps his fingers. 'Out you come, Laddy. You two as well.'

At least it's not the earring one, I think, as we follow him out into the front room. He's younger. He's cross all right, but quietly spoken.

'Just looking round, mister, not doing any harm. See, we haven't done nothin' at all.' Jimmy squats down and holds out his hand to the dog, Laddy, who immediately comes over and allows itself to be petted.

I stand there like a dummy. I feel so guilty I hardly dare look at the man. I do though. He's wearing a checked shirt, and has a tattoo on his arm: a rose with something winding round it.

'It's not your property, is it?'

My shorts are my property, and they're all wet and ripped, but I don't think I'll point this out to him.

'I didn't know it were anyone's,' says Jimmy. 'Just

thought it were abandoned.' I wish he would sound a bit more polite.

'Well, you thought wrong, didn't you? And you can explain yourself to the missus. She'll not be that pleased either.'

I have to say I am not that keen to meet the missus. And yet I can't help feeling that there's something curious about their being so ... so fussy about this old ruin. Did they know someone was hiding away here? Was that what it was? Perhaps we are going to get a chance to do a little bit of finding out after all.

So when Jimmy begins to protest that he's no right to make us do anything, I cut him short. He looks at me, and then shrugs. So we follow the gypsy over to the caravans, him walking ahead of us with the dog, occasionally glancing over his shoulder to see that we don't change our minds.

There are a few people about but they're all clustered round the caravan nearest the road. There's a van pulled up alongside it, and a couple of men have their bottoms sticking up in the air, their heads under the bonnet. I'm glad the kids aren't around; they would make it embarrassing, being marched in like this.

I ask the gypsy why he doesn't have a ring in his ear. He tells me to belt up and then bangs on the door of the centre caravan, the one that's a bit bigger and newer-looking than the others. 'Wait here,' he says and goes in. Jimmy has his hands in his pockets and he's half whistling to himself.

'Do you know who we're going to see?' I ask.

'If you'd done what I said, we wouldn't be standing 'ere about to see no one.'

'It's not my fault.'

'You should've run.'

I'm about to say, you can't always run away, but I don't. It occurs to me that I wouldn't like it if someone said that to me. Not that I do run away that much. At least I don't think I do. Instead I say, 'Thanks for getting the dog off me.'

'He weren't serious.'

Jimmy's in a mood so I'm going to have to do the talking, I can see that.

The young gypsy beckons us in.

'All right, Paul, off you go.'

The missus is the woman I saw yesterday, the one banging on the tin for the kids to come and eat. Now she's sitting behind a wide table studying us. The inside of the caravan isn't like I thought it would be: no glass ball, cards, or shawls and smoky lamps, instead the missus has a typewriter beside her, a stack of letters, and one of those portable phones. She is looking at us hard, Jimmy in particular.

'I know you, don't I?' Maybe she's not my idea of a gypsy queen but there's no doubt she's the one in charge. Her arms are bare and red and rough. Her hair is straw blonde but it's chopped short; it looks like matting. Her eyes are blue stones. She doesn't seem bothered when Jimmy doesn't answer. Instead she starts to fire masses of questions at us. What were we doing? Where do we live? Did anyone send us?

Did anyone send us? Who would send us? And to do what? Perhaps she's only partly serious. I do the answering though most of the time it's Jimmy she has her eyes on; and when I try to explain that we were wanting to find out about the woodkeeper and the girl, she steamrolls right across me.

'We don't like you sneaking round our homes. We've enough trouble on our plates at the moment without having to bother with little kids like you. Just you remember that this is our land . . .'

I can't get a word in edgeways, which is a bit unlike me really. I can feel myself opening and shutting my mouth like a goldfish.

'Who's that old woman then?' Jimmy says, right out of the blue. It takes me by surprise, and it takes her by surprise too. 'The one that looks like a witch. She was sneaking round the wood, spying on us. We wanted to know who she was, that's all.'

I nod. A major contribution.

'I know who you are. You're the badger boy, Flint.' I didn't know that was his surname; Flint like a pirate. I look at him. A very small pirate. 'Jim Flint, isn't it?'

'Yeah.'

'You've got some neck coming round here, haven't you? There are a few that would happily string you up.' Why? I glance at him but his face is blank. What did he do? The funny thing is she doesn't seem cross about this at all.

'I'd do it again, if I found them hurting the badgers.'

'Would you now? I believe you would.' She says it sort of thoughtful.

I'm lost. I don't want to talk about badgers. I want to know about the girl and the old woman and the cottage, and if we're not going to learn anything then I want to go home, but I don't quite have the courage to open my mouth again, not at the moment.

'I'll tell you something, Jimmy Flint, and you,' she says, turning for a moment to me. But she's interrupted by the door opening and the sulky young gypsy poking his head in. 'Fetchers are going, Ma. Hogger says he's going too.'

She gets up and goes over to the window. Jimmy and I look too. The van with the caravan hitched up behind is bumping its way along the track to the road where there's a small group of Uncle John's men in yellow hats standing beside a lorry. I see that a few of the children have reappeared and are watching the family leave. No one is waving, though, and when the van is on the road, they turn away and begin to play a game of tag as if nothing has happened.

'They would do anything for a hundred quid, that lot.' She turns away. 'All right, Paul, they can go and bad luck to them. Masterson's not pushing us out though.'

But I remember what Uncle John had said over our lunch. He will buy or bully till he gets what he wants. Just like with Mum.

To us, firmly but quite nicely, not shouting or anything, she says this: 'The old woman is our business, gypsy business. You leave her alone. And you don't mention her to anyone. Just forget about her, even if you see her again, forget about her. Do you understand?' I nod. And then her manner changes as she says to Jimmy, 'I wouldn't dream of inviting that Parker family back, not after their little boy got sent down for six months because of you. Come to think of it, he should be out by now. Bear that in mind. I've got nothing against you, nothing, but you keep to your side of the wood from now on, all right, Jimmy Flint? And you too, Jim's friend.'

She gives us a nod as if to dismiss us, then sits down at the desk and picks up her phone. I go to the door, but Jim stays put. 'We'll go where we like in them woods. Always have done and you can't stop us.' That took her by surprise; me too. 'But we won't go blabbing about that old lady. All right?'

For a moment I think she is going to bite his head off, but she just looks at him, as if she's making up her mind about something. 'All right.' And that's it. She dials and then as we are going out of the door I hear her saying, 'You get me Mr Masterson, double sharp . . .'

She needn't have bothered. As we come down the

steps of her caravan, a yellow van pulls into the camp. It has J. MASTERSON printed in thick black letters along the side. If it's Uncle John I don't want to be there, but Jimmy holds me back.

Three men get out. They are wearing those plastic hats that you see people round building sites wear. I can't think what good it'll do to them here; there aren't any buildings that will fall down on them, unless they go poking round the old cottage, but they don't head there but for the camp itself. They have those poles and sighting things that surveyors use and they start measuring out the camp.

'It's like they own it,' mutters Jimmy.

Another yellow van pulls up, and parks beside the first. Nobody gets out.

Meanwhile three, no four gypsies stroll over to the men who seem to be making a performance out of their surveying. There's a lot of arm waving and 'left a bit, Bert. Steady . . .' and all very noisy and, it seems to me, quite deliberately ignoring the watching gypsies. The men in yellow all look large. Perhaps that's why they're not worried. I'd be terrified – the ear-ringed gypsy is there, arms folded, talking to one of his companions. They move closer.

The man with the tripod backs into one of the gypsies. 'Out the way, squire,' he says.

'Who invited you here?'

Some of the women have joined the men and I can hear their angry muttering.

'We have council permission.'

'Get lost.'

One of the gypsies swipes at the tripod. Instantly four more men in yellow step out of the back of the van.

I'm frightened. There's going to be a full scale battle – you can feel the violence, thick and hard in the air.

I pull at Jimmy but he won't move. 'Deliberate,' he says.

'What do you mean?'

'Don't you see? Them builders want a fight. They're stirring it.' And they are. One's rolling his sleeves and grinning, another has a pick-axe handle resting in the crook of his arm.

It's me that runs this time. It seems that we get pulled in different ways, Jimmy and me. I don't want to see them all fighting and yelling; it panics me, just the feeling of it all about to explode – not the same sort of fear as with her, the old woman, more like when Mum and Dad were at their worst.

Jimmy hangs back, ignoring me, and I run and don't stop until I'm safe inside the trees. He isn't long following though.

'Nothing happened,' he says in answer to my look. 'I never seen anything like it. She came out, Mrs Smith, you know, waving her arms and shouting at them all, her own lot and them, and they backed off. I thought there were going to be a real war . . .'

'Is that what you wanted to see?'

'No, course not.'

'Didn't find out very much, did we?'

'We did.'

'We didn't.'

He pushes himself away from the tree he's leaning against and I get up. We begin to make our way back to the path.

'We found out that there's some secret about that old woman. I bet she's on the run or something. And we found out there's strife between them and the man your mum works for . . .'

'All right, Sherlock Holmes.' I don't feel like talking so I walk slower and slower until he is almost fifteen paces ahead of me.

It's nicer like this, just seeing the back of his head. It's cooler now, and the woods are quiet and shady. I can hear the stream up ahead, singing over the stones. It's been a full day, and I am tired but I don't mind. I think I shall stop at the pool and bathe my scratched leg.

To my surprise Jimmy is waiting for me at the stepping stones. I pass him by and walk on up to the Forge. He follows me. I sit down on the shingle and let the water run over my toes and then I wash the scrapes on my leg. Jimmy plonks himself down beside me and starts to unlace his runners.

'You know, I don't think I would have spoken

to Ma Smith like that if you hadn't been there.'

That takes me by surprise, I can tell you. One minute the show-off, the next Mr Modesty. 'Oh?'

'You don't ever get into real trouble, do you, Geoff? The fella yesterday wouldn't touch you, same thing today.' He sticks his feet into the pool beside mine. We sit there for a bit admiring our wiggling white toes.

'Katherine!'

That's not Mum's voice.

'Kathy!'

We both look round.

'Kathy!' The calling is monotonous, like a chant, the voice cracked.

'Is it your mum?' Jimmy's holding my arm. My mother!

'No.'

It's her, up on the flat-tops looking down at us, the old woman.

'Oh my lord.' Jimmy's voice is a whisper.

And then my name again, more drawn-out, like a sigh, dusty and old.

Chapter Ten

How does she know my name?

Jimmy's shoving his feet into his trainers, all the time glancing up at the rocks where she is.

How does she know my name?

'Jimmy?'

'What?'

'How does she know my name?'

She's standing right on the lip of the flat rocks. All black except for her hair which looks grey as lead and fuzzes around her face like a storm. Can't see her face properly because of the light behind her but she's staring, I know, with that same look, staring at me.

'Don't know.'

'Kathy!'

Again. I can only just hear her voice now behind the sound of falling water.

'Answer her. Go on, say something before she falls in.'

It's all right for him. She hasn't said his name. He shakes my arm. 'Say we're coming, Geoff. We can't miss her now. Go on, say it.'

'Don't push me.'

'Go on!'

I raise my hand and give a wave. She doesn't move. She has something in her hand. What is it? Then she takes a step along the edge, towards us.

'She's going to fall!'

'No, she's not.' Something tells me she knows this place, that she is a part of it.

'Kathy!'

'Geoff, go on.'

With all the pushing and hissing and calling, the panic that had gripped me is slipping away, and irritation is taking over. 'All right.' I give another wave, 'We're coming!' and then I follow Jimmy along the side of the pool, scrambling up to the rocks, losing sight of her as we claw through the trees at the edge. It crosses my mind that she'll be gone when we reach the top.

But she's there, in exactly the same place, still by the edge, still looking down to where we were.

And you know what she has in her hand? A plastic shopping bag. I don't know what I thought it might be, but not that. It's so ordinary.

Jimmy nudges me forward. And he was the one in such a hurry to get up here. Typical.

We approach her, but slowly, and not right up to her either, not so close that she can touch us. It wasn't just the light. She is wearing black, an old cardigan, thin at the elbows, and a black skirt that comes midway down her calves.

'Hello,' I say.

She turns sharply, as if she hadn't realized we'd moved from down by the pool to up here. Her face is white, dirty white, and her eyes, just for a moment, are startled and then before I can back away, she steps up to me and has my hand gripped in hers.

'Kathy.'

'Yes.'

You would think that she would have buckets to say after all that calling but she doesn't, she just holds my hand and looks, and I want to pull back but she tightens the pressure. I find I can't even turn my head away. 'It's not really Kathy,' I manage at last. 'No one calls me that. It's Katherine.'

Her eyes blink slowly, like an owl.

'We were looking for you,' adds Jimmy.

She looks at him, and then back to me again. 'In my home.' What a voice, hoarse and dusty – like an old room.

'Just looking,' says Jimmy, 'didn't do any harm.'

'Play.'

Is it a question or what she wants us to do? 'What? Here?' She still has my hand.

'Peter and Kathy,' she says. 'Always here.' Her eyes have lost their hungry look and seem sad, two green pools of sadness. She releases my hand and turns away.

What does she mean, Peter here? That time I was concentrating and sort of glimpsed him, like he was

94

on the far side of the road, had she seen him too? Was it possible?

She's standing with her back to us, head bowed, lost.

'Did you think we were people you knew, did you?' Jimmy takes her hand, very gently, and she half turns back. 'I'm not your Peter, am I?'

She moves her head, a faint no. Then why did she say 'Peter'?

'What's your name?'

She looks puzzled. That slow blink again.

'Your name?' he says.

'Molly.'

'Why're you with the gypsies, Molly . . . the travellers?'

But, as if she hasn't even heard him, she turns and begins to walk off, crossing the narrow gorge without a glance, so sure-footed you'd think she could walk these rocks blind. Nothing doddery about her.

Jimmy runs after her. 'Why you staying with the gypsies?' he calls. He's like a terrier at her heels. She pauses as he comes up beside her and I see her duck her head and say something to him but I can't hear either of them from my side of the gorge.

And then she's gone. Odder than thirty-two left-footed boots. That's what Dad used to say.

'You know what she told me?' says Jimmy after kangaroo-leaping the gorge. 'Said the wood was hers!'

'Is that what you asked her?'

'No.'

'Perhaps it does belong to her.'

'Don't be daft. I told you that the Vines own it.'

'She's living in that cottage, isn't she? Perhaps that's hers.' My mind's working at last.

'Could be. Let's ask up at Vines'. My dad might know and all, if I can get him to talk.'

Just before we get to our side, Jimmy asks me what I'm thinking about. Peter, I say, because I am, in between all the other thoughts about being late, and what should we try and get done on our project because (needless to say) we haven't talked about it at all. The truth is, Peter's always there, waiting for me to think about him.

'You shouldn't think about him. I don't think about my mum.'

That's his business but I don't say anything.

'And I don't think you can bring people back, neither.'

I don't want to talk about it.

We are at the wood's end now. There's the path and the stile and a thrush rooting through the scrub grass to our right. And there's our house, and Mum sitting down, catching this lovely afternoon sunshine, sketching.

Perhaps you can't bring people back, but there are always the 'what ifs', aren't there? Like, what if they haven't really gone away, which is what it feels like

96

with Peter. And what if Peter comes back in someone else's body and we meet and we recognize each other?

Mum looks up and waves.

Jimmy gives me a nudge. 'You going to ask me in for tea?'

It's my birthday soon. I tell him that and ask him to come then. He looks a little surprised. 'OK,' he says. 'See you tomorra.'

Mum's changed out of her office clothes and looks almost human. She tilts her head back to squint up at me. 'Was that James with you? Why didn't you ask him in for tea?'

Why's she so keen on him? He's not her friend. I tell her he's coming to my birthday party.

'That's a nice idea. You never normally want to do anything on your birthdays, Kate.'

That's true, but I'd like to this time.

I sneak a look at her sketch pad. I wish she would get a job that was to do with her drawing and painting but when I tell her this, she says we're better off as we are and that we have a chance of making ends meet now. She says this quite firmly, like she's trying to convince herself. At least that's what it sounds like to me. Then she closes the pad and stands up. 'Do you want some tea? You know it's five-thirty, don't you, and we agreed five?'

'Yes. Sorry. Perhaps I could have a watch for my birthday. A cheap one.'

She laughs. 'Perhaps. You made a mess of your legs, didn't you?'

I did – they're criss-crossed with scratches which feel hot and itchy. I hardly noticed them before, and I wonder whether I'll end up like Molly, wandering around with a shopping bag. Mum won't.

I notice that all Uncle John's flowers have gone. Didn't last, I'm pleased to say. The house looks better without them.

Is it tomorrow or the next day that we have the class trip to the building site? I wonder if I can get out of it.

A little later, I am standing by my bedroom window looking out at the wood (I always do now before getting into bed), when Mum comes in.

'You look a hundred miles away,' she says, taking Rabbit out of my hands. 'He's getting old, losing his hair.' She props him up on my bedside table. 'Were you thinking about Dad?'

'No.' In fact I was wondering how on earth me and Jimmy were going to make a decent map of the wood. It's so big. I was also thinking about her, Molly, and the way she'd called our names, Peter's and mine I mean; not that it meant anything.

'You had a good day then?'

I think Mum wants to talk but we somehow don't find the right things to say. She stays to tuck me in though, and I almost tell her about Molly. I want to but instead I say, 'Why can't you let us go all over the wood?'

'Oh,' she says, with that sort of bright 'it doesn't really matter' tone of voice. 'You remember the visitor we had, on the very first night. She was from the police. She told me that one of the patients from a Hereford Hospital, an old woman, had run away and they thought it was possible she might come to Bexstead. Apparently she used to live the other side of the wood. I was just being cautious, that's all.' She kisses me and turns out the light.

What sort of a patient runs away from a hospital? And from what sort of hospital do they run away? A prison hospital? Should I tell? Mrs Smith said we weren't to say anything about her. But should we? I bring Rabbit back into the bed and hold him tight.

CHAPTER ELEVEN

Normally I don't mind school. What I mean is it actually hasn't been so bad, what with the project and everything. People leave me alone – funny how a busy classroom can be quite peaceful at times, which was what it was like until Jimmy arrived.

He wasn't there for morning registration so I started to work on our map of the wood. Then he strolls in after the morning break with some stupid excuse that Miss Tracy accepted. Can't think why. And then he starts to criticize the map. I could really have punched him. I didn't though. We are meant to be a team. I just ignored him and then when I went to work at an empty desk he got in a right mood . . .

It's not true, what I've just been saying. It's not what really happened.

I was sent to stand in the corridor and I feel ashamed. Not because I was sent out by Miss Tracy, though I like her and feel sorry that she had to be cross with me, but because . . . because I have been horrid to everyone and I don't know why . . . and . . . I haven't been telling the truth, not strictly anyway.

This is difficult for me to talk about, especially after everything had been going so well. To be honest I wasn't going to say anything at all. I felt like stopping or just making everything up but then what would be the point in that? Lies are all right if you are telling stories – though I've given up doing that – but they aren't when you're hiding the truth. That's what I think, anyhow. I hadn't thought about it before but that is what I think now.

I woke up and my pillow was wet, soaked through. It happens sometimes, probably got a bucket of water inside my head and it leaks out. I swear I have no memory of why I cry. It doesn't happen that often, but it's always the same, I wake up and there I am, damp as a banshee on an Irish moor, and I always feel odd after it's happened, a bit snappy to tell the truth. At least I never cry when I'm awake.

What I did was get up, pull back the bedclothes, so that the top of the bottom sheet could dry off, and then since it looked like a good morning, I took my pillow down into the garden because it was sunny. I was going to leave it on one of the windowsills to dry.

Well all that was nothing; it was what I found on the doormat that upset me. There were two rabbits, baby ones, lying there, little white paws pointing straight in front of their noses. They looked sweet and their fur was so soft, softer than my Rabbit's, but when I picked one up I could see a thin black line across its throat. Dried blood. Puckered and hard. They were dead.

I didn't scream or anything stupid like that, and I didn't feel sick either. I brought them into the kitchen. Mum wasn't up of course, just as well or she'd have fainted. She makes a huge deal about being squeamish, almost as if she's proud of it. I don't think she is though. She knows all about hospitals and things like that. She must do because I can remember very clearly that she was in hospital herself for a long time after Peter died. I was never told what the matter was with her; she never said and nor did Dad. He and I used to visit, though I was the only one who talked. I talked about everything non-stop, because I hated their silence. It was when she came home that the rows started.

I put the rabbits on the table and then I wrapped them in newspaper and put them in the dustbin. A little bit later I emptied a waste-paper basket on top of them to cover them up.

There is only one person apart from Mum and Uncle John who knows I have Rabbit – Jimmy. He told me he used to trap them round the Vines' house so I knew it was him who'd murdered them. It was so horrible I didn't want to have anything to do with him at all, ever. And I was so upset that when Mum came down to have her cup of coffee and morning cigarette, I picked a fight.

I don't know why I do it. She does it too sometimes, I think, snapping at me when there's something else gnawing away at her. What I said was, 'Did Daddy leave because you were always going out with Uncle John?' Even as I said it I knew it was a poisonous thing to say. I could almost feel my nose and chin growing long and spiky like a nasty little witch.

'Is that what you really think?'

I didn't answer.

'That's a terrible thing to say.'

I know. I feel ashamed now to think of it.

Mum stood in the corner of the kitchen beside the kettle, half hugging herself, left hand gripping her right arm as if she'd been wounded, and smoking of course. I hate the stink of her cigarettes; they really get on my nerves.

We shouted a bit — at least I did — and then, predictably, I slammed out of the front door.

And then school was a disaster. I ended up punching Jimmy in the face, and gave him a nosebleed.

I was surprised at how easy it was to do something like that, and the class was impressed — nobody has hit Jimmy before and got away with it. But I'm not proud of myself at all; in fact I feel embarrassed.

I didn't punch him straight off. I suppose I hoped he'd say something that would make it all right, not that anything he could say would make those baby rabbits alive again, but anyway that's what I hoped. Of course he said nothing, nothing about the rabbits, but he was in a cheery mood and immediately wanted to see the map of the wood I'd started to draw. I showed it to him.

'Hey Geoff, that looks great,' is what he said.

'No, it's not. It's rubbish.'

'No, really you're a good drawer. The badger sett is over to the right a bit. Yeah. You going to come with me to Hereford, to the council offices? We'll get the map that shows all the boundaries and who owns what there. I can't believe that Molly woman owns it at all. I was thinking about it last night . . .'

'When you were out in the wood.'

'No, in my bed, thinking about her. She don't own it. What's she doing living like that if she do own it? Don't make sense.'

'When did you go out then?'

'The stream comes down a bit more there. Sorry. Sorry. I'll get on with my own bits. You don't half look odd this morning.'

That is how it went, sort of. I suppose I didn't come out with it straight away, the accusation I mean. Anyhow I didn't answer him and he shrugged and got on with his own work. But even that irritated me. Miss Tracy was delighted and fussed over him because he was sitting quietly, his tongue stuck between his teeth, laboriously writing. I wanted to know what he was writing but he didn't offer to tell and I certainly wasn't going to ask.

Then, as if he hadn't noticed me smouldering away for ten minutes, he said, 'I only went out to do the paper, the usual time, why?'

'Is that when you killed them?'

'What am I going to kill on my rounds, eh? What's got into you?'

'Rabbits,' I said. Sounds funny now, doesn't it. Lucky for him he didn't laugh, I would really have killed him if he had.

He looked at me a couple of times but I ignored him and got on with my map. Then a bit later he said, 'And I was thinking about your mum, you know, and my dad. It would be a laugh if they got married wouldn't it?' He said it as if it were just a funny thought that had come to him and it didn't mean anything. 'Make me and you brother and sister.' And he began to whistle quietly through his teeth.

Whamo! That's when I socked him smack in the face.

I have to hand it to him, he didn't go moaning to miss like the others would. He just rocked back on his chair, I thought he was going to fall off actually but that probably only happens in the films. And my hand really hurt too. In fact I think it was me going 'Ouch!' that got Miss Tracy speeding over. I bet you a million pounds she was ready to lay into Jimmy too – teachers are like that, even the nice ones; if someone gets a bit of a reputation that's them sunk. She did say, 'Jimmy!' in a shocked voice but I think that was more because of the blood gushing down over his mouth and dripping off his chin and on to his T-shirt. He looked so terrible I could only stare. Him too.

Of course she wanted to know what happened. He tried to say it was an accident but I wasn't going to have that. Don't ask me why. It is more my style to deny everything before the first question is asked, but this time I said it plain: 'Sorry, miss. I hit him.' She sent me straight out and then threatened to pack me off to the Head when I wouldn't tell her why. But it was none of her business. Well, it wasn't was it? And anyway I'm not sure I could have explained. I didn't really know why I'd done it anyway, not then.

I had to spend the rest of the morning standing in the corridor. I got very bored looking at the pictures and poems that had been put there for display. There was one about a badger that ended:

> *'Your jaw can snap*
> *a terrier's back*
> *easy as dreaming.'*

I didn't think badgers could be dangerous like that.

I had to have my lunch on my own in Mr Wootton's office and in the afternoon I had to work in the library. In fact I didn't really mind being on my own. At least I didn't have to talk about what I'd done. The other girls would have been round me like flies to know what was going on between Jimmy and me, and I might well have ended up punching one of them, which wouldn't have done me too much good. Miss

Tracy did come to see me. She wanted to know whether everything was all right at home. I said that of course it was.

I think I now know why I had one of those crying dreams. It must have been about Peter. Anyway I think Jimmy's right. You can't bring people back. I know that.

Jimmy was waiting to talk to me after school.

He didn't say anything about me hitting him and I tried not to look at his nose. 'What were you on about the rabbits for?' he asked.

So I told him.

'I wouldn't do that. I mean I don't mind hunting them but I wouldn't leave them like that for you because, well, I know, don't I . . .' He meant he knew I was odd and had a toy rabbit that I still liked but he couldn't get his mouth round the words to say it. I believed him.

I was still in a mood so I didn't offer anything. I certainly didn't offer him an apology for whacking him in the face.

I began to walk off back home. To my surprise he fell in beside me. 'Sounds like someone who knows how to trap them proper, with snares, you know. Someone who knows the wood too. A gypsy, I suppose . . .'

It was her!

I knew it was her then and I should have known

it before because of the way she had looked at me. She was mad. Mad as midnight and twice as dangerous. That's why they had been looking for her, the police. My first thoughts were that we ought to tell but then I thought if she is sick and mad and dangerous why had the gypsies made us swear not to say anything? It didn't make sense.

And why had she left that message of the dead rabbits for me? I was certain it was some kind of hideous message.

'Geoff,' said Jimmy, grabbing my arm and pulling me round. Without realizing it I had been storming down the street ahead of him. 'You're muttering,' he said. 'What's up?'

He had to shake me before I told him, and then it all came tumbling out. I was so frightened I didn't want to go home. She hadn't seemed so mad when we had met her – strange, but not mad; not much stranger than Mum but she doesn't go round killing things – well, she does actually but a plant killer isn't quite the same thing as what Molly had done. I knew what her message meant. She wanted to kill me because she thought I was some different Kathy, or because I wasn't the Kathy she wanted me to be . . . Oh, I didn't know what I thought. Except I didn't want to go home because I didn't know who would be waiting for me.

You know what Jimmy said? 'Don't worry!' I couldn't believe he could be so stupid. Of course I had to worry, I couldn't stop. 'Why me?' Over and over again, like a bluebottle buzzing against a pane of glass. 'Why me?'

'She's just an old woman,' he said. 'Won't do any harm, I reckon. Don't take on, Geoff, really. She won't hurt you. I reckon they were meant as a gift — for your dinner, you know . . .' He kept on, talking at me, soothing until I found I was actually listening to what he had to say. 'I think the gypsies must really believe that she do own the wood,' he said, 'and that's why they're willing to hide her. It's like she's their protection see, from Mr Masterson bulldozing it all down for more houses.'

It was a thought. 'Oughtn't we to tell?' I said.

'No.' He made me look at him. 'We promised. Now I'll take you home, all right?'

I nodded.

He walked back with me. There was nothing on the doorstep and Mum was painting in her makeshift studio in the garage; everything was sunny and normal.

'See you tomorrow then, Geoff,' and he was off.

I'm glad he didn't stay around for Mum to see him; his nose was still a bit red and mucky from the nosebleed. I don't think I'd be so forgiving if I were him.

Perhaps he gets thumped by the brother he hates so much that one punch on the nose from me doesn't mean anything. I hope so.

I sat up half the night by the window, Rabbit on my lap, looking and waiting for her to come across the lawn towards the house. I thought I saw something once but it could have been I was getting too tired and my eyes were playing tricks, because for a few seconds I did see a figure step out from the trees and stand in our garden and then when I blinked the figure was gone. I fell asleep in my chair. I didn't dream about anything but I woke up exhausted.

At breakfast I remembered that it was that morning we had the class trip to Uncle John's building site. I hoped Uncle John wouldn't be there.

'Don't chew your lip, Kate.'

'Sorry, Mum.'

There were two police cars parked in our estate outside number twelve where an elderly couple had moved in a few days ago. Mr and Mrs Bligh. They were out on the doorstep talking to the police officers as I walked past. Mrs Bligh looked very upset, perhaps she was embarrassed to have the police come round. I wondered if they had done something wrong, and then I reckoned they were probably just being told about Molly, like we had been.

I'm not going into the wood again.

CHAPTER TWELVE

'Masterson Developments', black on red, a smart tin sign on an ugly wire fence – probably should have a skull and crossbones on it. When Uncle John took me and Mum up here there was mud and mess, now there are strange concrete and brick mushrooms that seem to have bulged up overnight and there's more mud and mess because the trees have been chomped back further.

I don't know what everyone expected but we are all silent as the minibus bumps through to a little car park over by a cluster of Portakabins.

The minibus turned up at eleven o'clock to take the first group to the site and Jimmy still hadn't come into school.

'You're very quiet this morning, Kate.'

'Yes, miss.'

The boys behind me were talking about two robberies that had taken place in the village last night. Perhaps that was why the police had called on the Blighs. I hoped it hadn't been that; not much of a welcome for them.

'Do you know where Jimmy is?'

'No, miss.'

She looked worried which surprised me. A bit later I overheard her and Mr Wootton talking, something about the social services 'stepping in' and him having missed too much school.

'Did you apologize to him?'

'Yes, miss.'

I know. I hadn't.

'Good.' She glanced at her watch then called out the first fifteen pupils who were to go on the minibus – I was one and Jimmy should have been another. 'Bring notebooks and pencils. That's all you will need. OK, out you go.' On the way out she pulled me aside and said quietly, 'You'll have a word with him, Kate, won't you?'

'Miss?'

'About school and . . .' she hesitated, 'and keeping out of trouble.'

'Yes, miss.' Why should he listen to me? The reason he's bunked off is probably because I'm such an unreasonable, pig-headed, rude, and useless witch that he's decided he can't stand to be in my company for another second.

I wish he were here. I was going to apologize this morning. I was, and tell him what Mum said, that the old woman wasn't any old woman but someone who'd escaped from somewhere – and was really dangerous. The police wouldn't bother about her otherwise.

Then I suddenly wondered if he had mitched off to

be in the wood and then met her. She could chop him up. She could.

'Don't bite your fingernails, Kate.'

'Sorry, miss.'

Helen and Janine, her best friend with the strawberry patch, were whispering and looking across at me. They have not improved in the short time I have been here – some people don't.

Helen leaned over. 'Did you break his nose, do you think?' she said, all pretend concern. Janine giggled. 'Shut up, Janine.' And then to me again. 'Did he have to go to the doctor?'

'No.'

I turned away and looked out of the window. I never hit anyone before this place. Peter used to kick the door when he lost his temper, growl and then kick. Probably would have grown up to be an ace footballer.

We passed the Mill and the heavy dark mass of Old Wood loomed up on our left. Was he there, up at his favourite place, the sandy bank above the stream where he was supposed to go and take me badger watching? I couldn't understand how he could skip school just because he didn't feel like it. I remembered my first morning and him strolling in a couple of hours late and just some stupid joke by way of explanation. Didn't he mind getting in trouble? I could see my reflection scowling back at me.

*

The site manager, a Mr Brook, takes us up to the office, the upstairs of the only two-storey Portakabin on the site. We're given little yellow plastic helmets. He tells us we can keep them, a gift from Masterson Developments. The boys like the helmets. Helen, on the other hand, refuses to wear hers. 'I'll look silly, miss.' She's right, but then I think she looks silly all the time, largely because she has a way of holding her head tilted slightly as if she's always expecting someone to take a picture of her. I'm glad I'm not pretty.

While Mr Brooks is droning on, a bit like one of his dumper trucks, about the building and how careful they are being to preserve the natural beauty of the area (can he really believe that?), the boys have their hats on and are butting each other like rams.

But I am not listening to him, or watching them, I am looking out of the roadside window towards the gypsy camp where her house is. It looks like an invasion has taken place; I can hardly see the caravans for trucks and materials, and the paddock where the horses were has gone completely. There's activity there too but I can't tell what.

If the gypsies are forced out, will she leave too?

Even as I'm watching, a battered heap of a car is hauling out a caravan. A small group of yellow-hatted men on the verge stand aside as the car pulls up. Then as it edges from the track on to the road, one of them turns and boots the side of the caravan! Just like that. The car stops again but when the group of men begin to gather by the driver's door, it jolts off. The men saunter across the road and back on to the main site.

They shouldn't be allowed to behave like that.

Mr Brooks is coming to the end of his little speech when Miss Tracy cuts across him. 'What's going on over there?' I hadn't realized Miss Tracy had been watching the scene from the window too.

'What? Oh, a family moving on, I expect.'

'What were your men doing over there?'

He looks a little surprised by the sharp edge in her voice; surprised but not very bothered. 'Checking, I expect. We have to check every day for things that have gone missing.'

'And do you find anything?'

His answer this time is curt, 'Sometimes.'

'I see.' I don't think she believes him but she thanks him anyway, and then briskly organizes us into three groups of four. We have thirty minutes to go round the site and make notes. So that's what we do.

On our way back to the office, I spot Uncle John looking down from the window. I try to hide behind the others but of course he sees me right off. 'Kate!' He ushers us inside.

I can feel everyone's eyes boring into my back.

'What do you think, eh?' I'm about to tell him but he immediately draws in the rest of the group by saying, 'What do you all think? It will look really good, I can tell you that all right.' Perhaps he guessed what I was going to say.

Nobody says anything.

'It's perhaps a little hard to imagine,' says Miss Tracy.

'Of course it is.' And then he launches into his 'I have a vision' speech. I have heard it at home so it all sounds a bit fake but I suppose he's quite good because no one has actually vomited by the time he comes to the end, and the truth is Uncle John *will* have it neat and tidy in the end.

'What will happen to the gypsies?' asks Miss Tracy.

'They have to put up with change like the rest of us.' I can see Uncle John doesn't have much time for people like Miss Tracy. 'And they don't own the land you know.'

'Does this mean you are going to build over there too? In Old Wood?'

He smiles. His teeth are very white. 'There is no restriction as far as I know. If the owner wishes to sell, I would certainly consider a modest development there too. It would all mean more money and jobs for the village. Or don't you think that is important, Miss . . . ?'

'Yes,' she says, 'it is important, Mr Masterson, but there are other things that are important too.'

It's interesting seeing two grown-ups who obviously don't like each other having a polite row. Miss

Tracy is as cool as can be and tougher than I thought.

'Indeed there are,' says Uncle John. 'Perhaps you'd like to come and have dinner with me and we can talk about those "important" things.' He winks at the girls and Helen nudges Janine.

'No thank you, Mr Masterson.'

Uncle John laughs. A young man in a yellow Masterson coat and hat appears at the door. 'Now if you'll excuse me,' he says and turns to the worker. 'What is it?'

'Our friends across the road.' The young man jerks his head, indicating the gypsy camp, and smiles. He has a nice, easy smile, and a soft way of talking that makes me think he is local. 'Only three families left.'

Miss Tracy has started ushering us out but I just catch Uncle John's, 'Oh, what a shame!' before I'm out of the door and trotting down the steps after the others. The young man looks vaguely familiar.

Back in the classroom in the afternoon, fat Simon has a go at me for being friends with Uncle John. I knew it would happen. Miss Tracy hears but she doesn't say anything. They have all decided he's 'gross', even the ones who are not too bothered about what he's doing. I'm tempted to tell them that he's really a saint who spends all his free time working for starving children in India, but I don't. To make up something nice about him would make me feel ill. I feel ill anyway.

I'm now pretty sure who that young man at the

site office was, or at least who he reminded me of – the motorcyclist we saw talking to the fat gypsy. And Jimmy had said that the motorcyclist was his brother. Jimmy never said his brother worked for Uncle John.

If Uncle John's plans work out, he'll chop down everything, buy the house on the hill, and . . . I duck my head and say nothing to anyone for the rest of the day.

I wish Jimmy were here.

When I come out of the school gates I feel so low I reckon I could slither down the grate in the drain with no problem. I don't want to go home, not on my own, and so, without really thinking about it, I head in the opposite direction, towards Jimmy's. I have to warn him about missing school and the social services. And I have to say sorry for yesterday. I walk quickly, hoping that he hasn't stayed away because of me.

It isn't hard to find but then the village is so small you could find a pin in it easy enough. The garage is beyond the green, on a lane leading off the end of the main street.

It doesn't look like too many people use it. The forecourt has thick grass breaking through cracks in the tarmac, and the two Shell pumps with their shell-shaped heads are so eaten through with rust that they tilt slightly towards each other, like they're whispering. The garage itself is nothing but a rounded corrugated iron shed. Slap next door to it is the house, white but needing a coat of paint. The door is slightly open.

I wish Jimmy would come out. I ignore a stupid feeling that the pumps are sniggering at me, and walk across the forecourt and knock on the door.

There's no answer so I knock again. Jimmy has to be there. I push the door very slightly and hear someone muttering, and then there is a crack, like a chair falling over, followed by mumbling and shuffling that becomes more and more faint.

'Well, 'allo.'

I get such a shock I must look like a kangaroo the way I jump back from that door. The dark young man from Uncle John's site office is watching me from the door of the garage. He is still wearing his yellow hard hat, tipped back and to one side, and I have the sure feeling that he was waiting to see whether I was going to sneak into the house. I feel my face go red. 'Watcha doin' then, eh? Bit of spyin' on the old man?' He smiles. 'Or is it me you've come to see?' He is about twenty I suppose and handsome. He knows it too. Handsome is as handsome does. I don't know why that pops into my mind. 'Well?'

I don't think he likes the way I look at him. I can't help it but when I first meet someone I just look. It's not polite I know but it's what I do. He still has that easy smile on his face but it's what I call a practice smile.

I know who he is.

'You're Frank, aren't you?' I say.

'Tha's right.' He has a slight burr in his voice, not as strong as Jimmy's but then he had been away, Jimmy said, for about two years. He didn't say where Frank had been. Just that he didn't like him. 'Who are you?'

'Kate.' That doesn't register very much. I help him out: 'Jimmy's friend.'

'Oh, is that right? Jimmy doesn't say much about his friends.' He pauses. 'Maybe he thinks I'll steal them.' And he winks, like Uncle John. Some people like winkers. I can't say I do. He strolls past me. 'Come in. Perhaps the baby brother is round the back. Like a cup of tea?'

It's dark and messy inside, with spanners and tins of grease and rags around the place, as if the garage has managed to creep in through the door with no one noticing. The front room has a big old TV in it, a couple of armchairs and a thin strip of carpet. Beer bottles are stacked up in the fireplace.

There is a door off to the right. I hear the creak of someone getting up from a bed or an old chair. I suspect that everything in that house is old and ready to be thrown away.

'Frankie!' The voice is hoarse and soft.

'Yeah later, Dad.' Frank pushes the door shut with his foot. 'This way,' he says to me and goes through into a bright and clean kitchen. Someone has bothered to wash and tidy and sweep the floor. A mop and bucket stand in the corner by the back door. There is a dresser against one wall with some green cups and saucers stacked up on it, a large wooden table, and a window above the sink that looks over a yard.

'Dad's not too well,' says Frank, filling the kettle and putting it on. 'That's why I'm home, to look after him like.' He smiles round at me. He's lying. It seems so obvious to me I even wonder whether he wants me to know that he is lying, but why would anyone want to do that? There is no sign of Jimmy.

'I think I'll go home now.'

'Don't you want to see our Jim? I'm sure he'll be back any moment. Have a biscuit.'

Crunch creams. Sickening isn't it, but I'm a pig for certain sorts of biscuits. 'Thank you.' I take two in case he doesn't offer them again.

'Where's home? Don't tell me. Them new houses?'

'Yes.'

'Thought so. Fine houses, those are. Pricey I should think.' I don't offer anything. 'I know who you are now, Jimmy's friend. I do indeed. I've seen your mum,' he continues after a moment. 'Quite a looker, isn't she?' I concentrate on my biscuit. 'Your dad not live with you?'

'No.' I don't like his questions. 'Why do you want to know?' I think I sound a bit crumbly because of the biscuits.

He smiles and I decide I don't like his dark, handsome face or his pretend doggy soft brown eyes either. 'Just interested,' he says. 'You're friends with the boss aren't you, you and your mum? And that's one of his houses you live in –'

I interrupt him. 'What's the matter with your father?'

He pours the tea. 'Oh, getting old mostly,' and he pushes the mug across the table and offers me another biscuit. 'Wouldn't mind one of them houses,' he continues, it's more like he's thinking aloud than talking to me.

No, I don't like him at all. 'You're trying to get rid of the gypsies, aren't you?'

'Me? Why d'you say that?'

I'm sure he was one of the men round the leaving caravan that morning and I recall how it was him we had seen coming into the camp on the motorcycle that first time we sneaked up there.

'Is that your job, to get rid of them?'

'The boss likes getting things done. Like in the army.'

'He doesn't own the wood though, does he?'

He ignores that. 'Frank Flint,' he says, lighting a cigarette. 'Private 99000230. Could have made it to corporal easy if it hadn't been for Dad.'

As if he has overheard him, his father calls weakly from the front room again. Frank hesitates, then pushes back his chair with a sigh and slopes down the hall. 'All right, you can wait five minutes can't you?' There is a mumbled reply and then I hear Frank saying, 'You've had enough to float a battleship but I'll nip out in five minutes and get you some. I said I would so don't fuss. Right?' He reappears and leans up against the door.

I stand up to go.

'Not leaving are you?'

'Yes.'

'Did the boss give your mum that house?' I don't answer. 'I bet he did. And what's he get in return, I wonder?' I don't turn away but my eyes prickle a bit.

'Perhaps the boss will give me a house if I do him a few favours.'

I wish I could put a spell on him. Fat chance; I can't even turn a tadpole into a frog. 'I'd like to leave now, please.'

'Who's stopping you? Remind me to Mr Masterson the next time he comes visiting your mum.' He doesn't move out of the way, so I have to push past him. Then I run out of the front door. I don't stop running until I am at the end of the lane.

CHAPTER THIRTEEN

Without even thinking about it, I head for the swing on the green.

A small group of boys saunter on to the green at the far end and begin to kick a ball around. I don't see Jimmy. They had better not kick their stupid ball anywhere near me.

The green dips sideways and then crazily back again as I give the chains that hold up the swing a savage twist.

Two girls from the baby class come up to me on the swing. 'You're Katy Gaveston, aren't you?' They both have bunches and eyes like saucers. They have a dog too. It pees on the iron leg of the swing.

'No, I'm not.' My eyes itch.

'You are too.' But she looks unsure. 'Can we have a go?'

'No.'

I watch them wander off, the old dog trailing behind them. The clock on the church begins to chime. *Dedong / Your time / is up / Kate Gav / eston.*

And then, quite suddenly, I know what to do. Find Mum a new job, of course.

How can I?

There's a shout from down the green and the ball comes rolling towards me, practically stopping at my feet. I give it a hack that hurts my toe but which, quite astonishingly, sends the ball whizzing back to the boys. 'Oh yah!' shouts one of them. I take that as a compliment.

Perhaps if I telephone Dad . . . It's a thought. Not a very good one but it *is* my birthday soon and Dad usually phones on my birthday and he could talk to her . . .

The day begins to feel better.

I wish I knew where Jimmy was.

I cross the road and, on impulse, turn into the churchyard through the little lych gate with its sloping moss-covered roof. I hope Jimmy and I are still friends. I'm not sure that I know how to say sorry so that it sounds real.

The churchyard is shaded by two huge trees of dark, dark green. The place feels old and still and cool, a bit like the wood. The graves all seem well kept, even the very old ones. I like that, the fact that someone cares for them.

One of the inscriptions reads 'Albert Flint' – I wonder whether he was some relation to Jimmy. '1822–1899. Let him walk surely the dark night.' What a thing to write. All it said on Peter's was 'Our much-loved son'.

There's a funny drawing carved at the bottom of

the inscription but it's partly covered with lichen. It looks a bit like a trap.

'Let him walk surely the dark night.' I like that.

'And what do you think of my friend Albert?'

I practically jump out of my skin. I don't know what I thought. A voice coming out of one of the graves it sounded like. Of course it's only Mr Smallwood, the vicar, looming over me. I normally don't like adults who loom and who wear funny clothes.

'I'm sorry. I didn't mean to startle you.' I've met Mr Smallwood in school but I didn't think he'd know who I was. But he does. 'You're the Gaveston girl, aren't you?'

'Kate.'

'That's right. I remember now.' He isn't wearing that white cloak thing vicars wear so I suppose he isn't going to give a service. Mum and I don't go to church because Mum says she doesn't believe in God. She wanted to cremate Peter. Dad and I wouldn't let her.

'I like what they said about Albert.'

He smiles when I say that. He doesn't look like a priest. I mean he has that collar but they all have that, it's just that he's not balding with a droney voice. His hair is silvery grey, wisping out over his ears and his eyes are very dark. 'Yes. I've always liked it too.' He squats down beside me and absently plucks weeds from the rounded lozenge mound of Albert's grave.

126

'Did you make it up?'

He laughs, but not sneering, even though when you come to think of it it's a pretty stupid question. He would've had to have been about a hundred years old even to have been a baby when Albert popped off. 'I've often wondered what Albert did for a living. What do you think he did?'

'I don't know. Perhaps he was a poacher.'

'I hadn't thought of that. The dark night, eh? Keeping out of the mantraps? They used to set them here, up in the wood. Huge steel traps, could crush a man's leg.'

I am impressed that he knows about things like mantraps. I wonder whether Jimmy knows. 'What do you think the writing means?'

'A gardener, that's what I always thought. A gardener who sang songs in the evening. Not so logical. Are you waiting for someone?'

'No.' He asks me a bit about home and Mum. I like talking to him. He knows the village. I don't mean where everything is but he knows it under its skin. We start walking back together and he tells me about the Vines and how they used to own everything for miles around, which is what Jimmy had said. He tells me about the gypsy camp too and how, ever since the last keeper married a gypsy, there had been a couple of families living on that plot of land at the edge of the wood. He tells me the ruined cottage belonged to the keeper's daughter, a poor old thing whom he visits in a hospital in Hereford whenever he can.

Bam!

'Is her name Molly?'

'Molly Birkin, that's right. How did you know that?'

'Does she own the wood?'

We are standing at the lych gate about to go our separate ways. He looks puzzled when I ask him this. 'No, not as far as I know. It's still Vine land,' he says thoughtfully. You know, as if expecting me to tell him something more. So I do.

I tell him that I think the gypsies had hoped that Molly really did own the wood and that it would stop them being driven off by Uncle John. 'You know she's living in the wood,' I say. I know I promised Mrs Smith, at least Jimmy did, but Mr Smallwood is a priest.

'Yes,' he says. 'Yes, I was told.'

Mr Smallwood seems to be concentrating but I gradually get the feeling that it's not exactly on what I'm telling him. 'Did she kill someone?' I ask.

He looks startled. 'Molly? Goodness me. Well now, her father was said to have been poisoned but nothing was ever proved. And that's all a very long time ago, Kate. A very long time ... Poor Molly, living in the woods. I ought to find her.'

'She might kill you.'

'No. No.'

'If she did own the wood, Mr Masterson and his men would like her out of the way, wouldn't they?'

'They might. They might indeed.'

And that's it. Perhaps he is thinking about his next sermon or something. I expect that happens to priests – right in the middle of chatting they suddenly remember that they have to make up something very long for Sunday. I don't think it rude of him to go quiet. I go quiet sometimes.

We make our goodbyes. He shakes my hand and invites me to call in on him for a cup of tea any time I like. His hands aren't soft at all. I bet he gardens the graveyard. I wonder whether he is married.

Jimmy is in the garden cutting the grass with Mum's new mower, flying up and down, his shirt stripped off and a baseball cap I haven't seen before twisted back to front. He has made a flower bed by the gate and another one over by the front door. I can't believe it. He'll have Mum eating out of his hand, that's for sure. He looks funny, zipping up and down, so skinny and small. I really hope I haven't broken his nose.

'Hi!' I'm over by the gate but he doesn't see me, or at least pretends not to. I practically have to lie down in front of the mower to make him stop. 'Hi.'

'Geoff!' He rubs his wrist across his forehead. 'Just want to finish this, all right?' And he's off again and all I can do is step to one side. He doesn't look so funny close up. It's not his nose, that looks fine. He just looks serious, or maybe anxious. I don't know, perhaps I'm wrong, perhaps it's me because I don't feel very comfortable having to say sorry. I notice he has a livid bruise on his arm, like it has got caught in something.

I dump my bag inside the house and pour out two juices, slide in two cubes of ice, and bring them out just as he's pushing the mower over to the garage. 'Thanks. Wait a sec,' he says, pulling his shirt on before taking the glass.

We don't look at each other while we're sipping the drinks. At least I don't look at him. It's not that I don't like saying sorry – well, now I come to think of it, I don't much – it's more how you say it. 'Sorry about the nose' sounds stupid. 'I didn't mean to' (always my first choice) is a lie.

Funny thing is we both start talking at the same time.

'Your arm hurt?' (That's me.)

'Lost your rag, didn' you?' (Him.)

'Yes, sorry.' (Me.)

'Nah.' (Pause.) 'Caught in a door.' (Him.) 'Wait a minute. What did you say?' (Him again.) 'My ears not deceiving me?' (Him.)

'What?' (Me. Suspicious.)

'Did you say sorry, Geoff? Did you?'

In my opinion some people can be totally unreasonable. He grins until I tell him about my visit and meeting his brother. That buttons him up tight. And because I'm still peeved, I give him a heavy warning about the social services and not bunking off school or they'll put him in a home.

'I don't care if they do take me away.'

'To go into a home?'

He shrugs when I say that. But he can't know what it means. I don't think I know either but it's the words, isn't it? 'Going into a home' is like a deep mine. I bet that's where they are, deep underground. He's in a funny mood. He won't tell me why he's doing all the gardening for Mum. She never asked him to, I know that, and he's hardly listening when I tell him about meeting Mr Smallwood, the vicar, and finding out about the keeper's cottage and Molly.

'I bet she's all right, that old woman,' he says. 'Cruel to lock up any creature in my opinion. Better to kill it.' He pushes the mower back to its place beside the garage. When he comes back to me he says, 'Do you think your mum will like them two new beds I made?'

The lawn now resembles a lawn and the beds are neat and the earth is rumpled and chocolaty dark. 'Yes.'

Right out of the blue he says, 'Can I stay the night?'

'Why?'

He shrugs. 'Just a thought. It don't matter.'

Some timing. Mum is stepping down the street and in through the gate, tastefully smart, *click-clack* in her neat shoes. Will this be me when I grow old? Not unless they invent a machine for rebuilding skinny bodies, knobbly knees and faces that naturally frown, into something that can fit in a grey suit.

Jimmy nudges me. 'Ask her.'

She would love him to stay. 'How nice to have a man around the house.' Jimmy glows like a torch. I'm getting stomach cramps with embarrassment. She kicks off her shoes and then barefoot she pads round the garden getting Jimmy to explain all his plans.

In fact it doesn't work, him staying the night. Not because of Mum. Not directly anyway. It's just that she insists on phoning Jimmy's dad, and Frank answers. The long and short of it is that Frank calls round to collect him. 'Can't do without our Jim. Maybe another time.' He's on the doorstep and I know in my bones that he is dying to be invited in to have a look around, and he's acting so smooth with Mum it makes my skin crawl. But she doesn't invite him. She's not rude but just acts as if she's busy, you know.

'I'm so sorry, James,' she says. 'Perhaps another night.' I don't know why Jimmy doesn't ignore his brother, but he's totally different when Frank is around, just his head down the whole time, looking at his trainers.

Before Frank arrived I'd asked Jimmy if he always did what his brother told him. It wasn't as if Frank was his dad or anything; but he just said he always had to and that was that. I don't think that's right. I don't think you should have to do something just because someone older than you tells you to do it, even if it's your mother.

Mum turns back to Frank. 'Are you sure he can't stay? I think we'd feel more secure with him in the house. Our neighbours were robbed recently.'

'Yes,' says Frank. 'I heard there's been a lot of burglaries round here. Damn gypsies, so everyone reckons. I don't mind stopping over if you like, Mrs. I was in the army you know, so you wouldn't have anything to fret about. And my father needs our Jim, 'cause he's a great little nurse.'

I've never seen such a look as Jimmy gave his brother. It was like he was shuddering, only inside where you can't see. But I see it though. Mum and Frank don't. Frank's standing cool and easy, one foot up on the front step, thumb hooked into the pocket of his black jeans and a pack of cigarettes – one of the black shiny packs – and a lighter in the other hand. I think he's still pretty sure that Mum will ask him in for tea or a drink. The bee's knees – that's what he reckons he is.

'No,' says Mum. 'I wouldn't like you to stay.' And then in a softer voice. 'Goodbye, James.' I am impressed.

Frank gives a little laugh. 'Suit yourself. Maybe another time.'

'I don't think so.'

'Come on then, Jim.' He grips Jimmy round the back of the neck and sort of steers him round.

Mum steps back from the door but I linger and I see Frank, just as they are going through the gate, pinch Jimmy's neck so hard that Jimmy jerks forward and nearly falls before angrily knocking his brother's hand away. 'Leave off!' I hear him say.

Frank raises his hands in mock surprise, taking a step back as if Jimmy might thump him. 'I was only joking.'

I wish Jimmy had thumped him.

If Jimmy had stayed he'd have helped me face up to her about her job. Probably would have said, 'You don't want to work for that man Mrs G., he's not good enough for you.' 'Why's that, James?' 'Well, because he's fat for one thing and for another he's going to ruin all the village, and because he likes to have people like our Frank working for him.' And she would have listened to him. She wouldn't be offended at all. I bet Peter would say things straight like that too.

Still I do try to put a part of my plan into action by phoning Dad. We haven't spoken since before the move. He used to telephone quite often, though Mum would never speak to him, she would hand the phone straight to me with a 'Yes, she's here.' I hated that, like opening the door to the fridge. Not that he ever had very much to say to me but I know I'm not an easy person to talk to. Mum is always telling me that so it must be true.

'Oxton 35653. Hello.' It's a girl's voice.

'Can I speak to Mr Gaveston?'

'Who's speaking, please?'

I have half a mind to put the phone down. What is she doing there? Who is she? Who is she to ask who am I? I stop myself skittering round in tight circles. 'His daughter.'

Clack. The phone is dumped on to a table. 'Mum,' I can hear the little creep calling, 'it's someone for Tony. Says it's his daughter.' A muffled reply from somewhere outside the room. Another click and then Dad's voice comes on. 'Hello, Katherine.'

It is not, I have to say, the most successful conversation we have had. I try to tell him about Mum but I don't think he's really listening. He doesn't even remember that it's my birthday coming up.

Don't worry, I don't burst into floods of tears. Mum often wishes I would. Don't ask me why. I'm not that upset by Dad. I've sort of known for a long time really that he's out of reach. I didn't like that little girl being there, though.

Uncle John turns up at six o'clock. I watch him half running up the garden path carrying a large cardboard box. He looks weird because all I can see are his scuttling legs, the box and his hairy hands clutching the sides. I can't see his head at all. Another present.

'Oh John, you really make it very difficult for me to say no.' I glare at Mum. There's nothing difficult about the word no, she must have used it at least one million times to me alone.

'Nonsense, Megs. It was a bargain.' He is bowed over a space-age, flat screen, black television. I've been dying for a TV but Mum always says they're a waste of time and money, and only lazy, uncreative people like slumping in front of them. 'Right, this goes in here,' he grunts, burrowing down behind the television. Then he straightens up, dusts his hands together, plugs it in and then points the remote control thing at the screen. A red light glows on. 'What do you think about it, Kate?'

'We've always managed without one before now.'

'You surprise me.'

'Mum said they were a waste of time and money and only –'

'That's enough, Kate.' I can hear the steel warning in her voice and shut up. To Uncle John she says, 'It's very generous, John. Thank you very much.' Mum kisses him on the cheek.

I find myself watching her like a hawk all through dinner. She's relaxed and friendly with him but I notice her twisting her white-gold wedding ring round and round her finger. I make a point of being polite all through the meal and only speak when I am spoken to.

After we've cleared away, Uncle John brings out a

map of the village and wood, and he shows Mum everything he's going to do. His development is circled in red and a big chunk of the wood, including where the camp is, has diagonal blue lines across it. That's because it is next, he explains. He raises his glass. 'To Mr Vine, to Mr Peter Vine for so kindly agreeing to sell me half of his estate, with planning consent, at a knock-down price like the regular knock-down gentleman that he is.' He laughs. She smiles. I don't think she realizes just what all this means.

The only good news is when he tells us that once he's concluded his deal with Mr Vine he'll be off abroad for a while on business. 'So if you want a job in Spain, Megs, just let me know.'

'I don't think so, John.'

She lets me stay up till he leaves. As soon as he is gone I pluck up my courage and I tell her everything, starting with the gypsies and how Jimmy's horrible brother is up to something bad and, whatever it is, he's doing it for Uncle John, and I tell her that her job is ruining her and that she should be painting.

There's a moment when I think she'll do her Italian volcano bit but she doesn't. Not even a simmer. 'Did you say anything of this to your father?' I shake my head. This is nothing to do with Dad.

At the end of it all she doesn't say she won't see him any more but nor does she row with me. She listened to everything I said. I think this is the first time that's ever happened.

I don't feel like going to sleep so I decide to do some work on the project, but I just write rubbish: 'The wood is very old and is made up of a mixture of deciduous and evergreen trees...' I write two pages of this, read it through and tear it up. It has nothing to do with the wood. I begin again. 'In the middle of the wood is a deep, dark pool. People say a beautiful girl was found drowned in it. She had long fair hair,' (I made up this bit) 'and looked like Ophelia. The pool is haunted by her sad ghost...'

It's not till much, much later, when I am sitting up in bed with Peter's picture on my knee and my diary open, that I remember something Uncle John said. Peter Vine. Mr Vine's first name was Peter. Molly called Jimmy and me Kathy and Peter. Perhaps she had been friendly with Peter Vine when they were young and Kathy was the girl, the sister, who drowned. We reminded her of the two children she used to know. Could that be it?

Even after I turn out my light, the little pieces of the story of Molly and her connection with the Vine family slide about in my head until gradually, just before I drift off to sleep, I figure out what the real story must be.

CHAPTER FOURTEEN

It was because I was thinking about it last thing before going to sleep that I dreamed about her. Except it wasn't her but her voice, calling over and over through the darkness, 'Kathy! Peter!' And there were two children but I couldn't see them properly, just the paleness of their faces in the dark. I thought I might have been one of them. I recognized the voice. I would never mistake it; raw, hoarse as the wind moving through winter trees. Odd to think that, with it being mid-summer, but there you are; I can't stop thoughts slipping into my head, no more than I can stop words, invariably the wrong ones, popping out of my mouth.

I wake up to the sound of rain whispering against the glass of the window and Rabbit with his nose next to mine. It hasn't rained since we came here.

My theory is this: It's not me she's calling, not really. It's them, the Vines, Peter and his sister who drowned in the Forge, Katherine, that *has* to be her name and that's who she sees. I don't mean actually sees them of course, but that there must have been something about Jimmy and me that made her think of them. Well, she is batty as a baked walnut, Mum said so, and having been locked away for all those years there's no wonder that she has that terrible voice.

Now what I think is that the Vine children came down and played in the wood. The Forge was probably their favourite place, and she, living in that cottage with her keeper father, used to spy on them, spied on them for ages without them noticing her at all. I can see her doing that, peering out at them from the bushes. I bet she was always a bit mad. I can imagine her as a little girl – brown skin and wild black hair, shiny coal black, and eyes that could stare through walls a hundred miles thick. Eventually she comes out and, although their family is posh and hers isn't, they begin to play, because children will get on together even if the parents are stuck-up and stupid. They become friends. She is able to tell them lots of things about the wood. They grow up and then this is what happens: Peter and Molly become lovers and he promises her the wood. 'My darling, the wood will always be yours.' Something like that. But it doesn't end happily at all, not at all. Kathy Vine is jealous and one day she tells Molly that her brother will never be allowed to marry someone like her, because she is half gypsy. And Molly, in a fit of crazy madness, strangles her with her incredibly strong hands, her long fingers reaching almost all the way round Kathy's slender neck, and so she kills her friend. She doesn't mean to but when you are half mad you do things that you don't mean to do. And, crying softly, she slides Kathy's body out into the Forge pool so that it will look as if she drowned.

Kathy's body is found by Molly's father, and so she poisons him, and then, unable to keep her terrible secret, Molly confesses to the murder and is locked away. Now all the time she is locked away the gypsies still stay on, believing that they have a right to that bit of land, because she told them that the forest was hers, given to her by Peter Vine.

Rabbit is quite impressed.

I get up and dress.

It's Saturday.

At home, in London, when I looked from my window, there'd always be people walking down the road. Always. And usually they'd be hurrying, even late at night, never dawdling, heels against the pavement. I don't miss that at all, but it's just that when I look out of my window now, I never see anyone. And yet I can't help looking for that shape in the trees that means she is there, watching. I'm sure she's not but that doesn't stop me looking.

Mum is sitting in the kitchen with a stack of brown envelopes in front of her. I know what they mean – who doesn't? 'We could sell the television,' I suggest helpfully.

Mum gives me a warning look.

'We could.'

'Oh yes, and I could fly to the moon. What I need is a . . .' she lets the sentence trail away, looking out towards the garden.

'Commission for a painting?'

'That'd be nice.' Then she sighs. 'Kate, do you really think I should stop working for John?'

'Yes,' I say, 'I think you should.'

She shoves back her hair and then reaches for her cigarettes. 'Not to put too fine a point on it,' she says dryly, lighting up and noisily inhaling, 'we need the money from that job. We really do.' She picks at a broken fingernail. 'Even these burglaries are getting me down. It's harder than London. It's not like I thought it would be down here. It really isn't.' She stubs out the half-smoked cigarette and gets up and then stalks up and down the kitchen like a cat swishing its tail.

I have my three cereals and think about this.

I think she must be lonely because I suppose it can't be easy living with me. 'I know I'm not much company,' I say eventually.

She stops her pacing. 'What makes you say that?' Her voice has a funny husky quality.

'I know I'm not,' I say. 'It's just a fact. I don't suppose you'd get back together with Dad? I did speak to him, you know.'

She looks at me as if I have landed from planet Zob; I probably have.

'He's not much good, I know,' I say. 'And I think he is with someone else. A girl answered the phone.' Perhaps I have said too much.

She gives a short laugh. 'No, your father wouldn't be much good. I'm sorry.'

I shrug. Well, I'd worked that much out for myself.

'I'll think of something,' she says.

'So will I.'

She smiles.

In fact neither of us do; Jimmy does. I see him coming up the garden path and I bang on the window and signal him to come in. I'm dying to tell him my theory about Molly and Mr Vine. I'm not so sure how much to say about Mum.

He's in a chirpy mood, carrying our newspaper and a large lump of wood that must have been extremely difficult to manage on his bike. 'Look,' he holds up the wood. 'Here you are Mrs G., you got a job if you want it.' He grins like a cat. His right hand looks a mess, all the knuckles are raw, skin peeled right off them. When he catches me staring, he dumps the slab of wood on the table and shoves his hands deep into his denim jacket pocket. He doesn't wince, though I'd have thought that would have been sore enough. He really does seem pleased with himself.

'What is it, James?'

What it is, is the shop sign of Mr Padden the

butcher, which once, according to Jimmy, had a very sad-looking pig staring out from its flat surface. Now the board is so weathered, all that can be seen is the faint outline of a pig's nose. Jimmy persuaded the butcher that he had a 'friend' who would do 'a right job', for which, if he were totally happy, Mr Padden would pay fifty pounds.

I am impressed. So is Mum. In fact, she says that if Jimmy were a little taller she would seriously consider marrying him. I think she is overdoing it rather, but he goes very pink and shuffles his feet like a baby in reception class. I am tempted to say that fifty pounds isn't that much, but in fact I think it's a huge amount. Anyway I mustn't be so churlish, as Mum says, and give credit where it's due. 'I seen you painting,' says Jimmy, 'and Geoff's always saying you're so good, I thought it would be handy.'

I don't remember complimenting Mum ever; she looks at me a little surprised. It's now my turn to study my toes.

'Well, I know what I shall do this morning.' Mum is all brisk now. 'What about you two?' Before Jimmy can object I announce that he and I must make some progress with our project, and then go up and interview Mr Vine about the wood.

'You're not trying to interfere with John's plans are you? You know he intends to buy Mr Vine's wood, and his house too.'

'No.'

'Kate?'

'No.' Of course I want to but I don't see how we can at the moment. No, all I'm hoping to do is to dig out the real story about the drowned Vine girl, and why Molly claims to own the wood. Still, if I get a chance to spike Uncle John's deal, I will. Mum is giving me one of her looks and I know she doesn't fully trust me despite our chat.

'He won't want to see us anyway,' says Jimmy. 'He's right stand-offish. That's what they say in the village.'

'As long as it's just to do with your project, I'll speak to him. I think I can arrange it easily enough. I was on the phone to him yesterday for John. Now if you two will give me an hour, I'll sketch out the design for Mr Padden's pig sign and we can all go into the village together. If he likes what I'm going to do, I'll treat us all to a trip to Hereford. How about that?'

Mum disappears to the garage studio while we go up to my room where I tell Jimmy my full and slightly embroidered account of the tragic tale of Molly and Peter, featuring the gruesome drowning of the inter- fering Kathy Vine.

He listens closely, perched up on my bed, chin in his hands. 'That's good,' he says. 'Did you make it all up?'

'Pieced it together,' I tell him. There is a difference.

'Doesn't work though, does it?'

'Why not?'

'Well, why would he give her the wood if she went and killed his sister?'

He has a point. 'I bet I got some of it right.'

'Maybe.' He grins.

He's different from yesterday, not so zippy – or frightened. Did he think his brother was going to do something to him? Or maybe make him do something he really didn't want to do? What? When I ask him what's going on he claims he doesn't know what I mean. And when I press him he says he reckons that something I said yesterday was right, that you shouldn't always do what you're told.

When Mum comes in she shows us her drawing. I wish I was clever at drawing. I should be because I seem to remember Dad being clever too, doing little sketches. Of course he needed to be good for his architecture. I suppose Peter inherited it all. I remember him scribbling in the kitchen. Fierce he was, gripping the pencil like a dagger. I can't say that I thought he was much good. Mum and Dad used to 'ooh' over him. He always said 'See!' when he'd finished, like there was really something to look at instead of a squiggle. Perhaps there was and I just couldn't see it.

What Mum has drawn is another pig, but it is the most grinning pig you ever saw, with a crown of laurel leaves perched on the side of its head. I think it will put you off eating pork for life but Jimmy says Mr Padden will love it.

Before leaving, Mum makes the phone call for us to Mr Vine and to Jimmy's surprise he says he will be there and we can come up in about an hour. We agree to go with Mum to the butcher's to give her a bit of moral support, and then cycle on up to the Vine house afterwards.

Jimmy's right, Mr Padden does love it. He loves it so much, he pulls fifty pounds out of the till and gives it to Mum there and then and tells her she could make a grand living painting signs all round and about. Mum is delighted and very giggly. I think Mr Padden rather fancies her, to tell you the truth.

Mum wants to go straight over to the pub, The Green Dragon, to ask about their sign while Jimmy and I want to cycle up to the Vine house, and so we part.

CHAPTER FIFTEEN

It takes ages to cycle up the long hill from the village to Mr Vine's house. It was much easier in the car; I was hardly aware of the hill then.

The first part of the climb is all cramped in by the trees on the edge of the wood, and then it opens up into grazing land; wide folding fields of green. And there, like it's stuck on the top of the world (or at the end of the world), are the two huge pillars holding up black and rusting gates. The gates are angled open and look as if they can't have been shut for a hundred years there's so much long grass and thistle growing through them. The road leads right through the pillars and up to a great lump of a grey house – the Vines'.

I wouldn't want to live here, even with that view. The house is long and sulky, the windows dark and frowning. A climber is spread over one end, the only bit of colour on the place, a fiery red, but it looks more like a raw patch on the face of the house than decoration.

It's so quiet up here, it makes me nervous and I begin to wonder whether Mr Vine has guard dogs. It's just the sort of place that would have massive dogs with eyes red as burning coal, and long dribbles of spit hanging through their yellow teeth. Hounds of the Vines.

'Jimmy?'

'What?'

I find myself edging a bit closer to him.

'What are you doing?'

I wish he wouldn't always push.

'Do you think it's safe?'

'Course. It's only Mr Vine up here. What did you think – Count Dracula or something?' He laughs.

As far as I'm concerned it's just the sort of place that you'd get vampires, or ghosts or mad dogs or the whole lot all wrapped up together. But vampires and ghosts don't bother me, just dogs. And Jimmy's good with dogs. I give a careless laugh to show I wasn't being serious.

'I wish you wouldn't do that.'

'What?'

'Laugh.'

Friends are meant to put up with their friends' defects. I can't help my laugh.

We lean our bikes up against the wall beside the porch and then go up the three steps to the door.

There's no knocker, just an iron bell pull which Jimmy yanks. We hear the ringing somewhere in the depth of the house and then a long, thin, elderly man in tweeds pulls open the door. 'The children,' he says thinly, but he might as well have said 'the dogs', there is so little interest in his manner.

'I'm Katherine Gaveston. My mother telephoned. And this –'

'In. In,' he says impatiently, talking right across me, which I think is so rude. He ushers us in with a fussy little gesture of his hand. If he didn't want us, why did he agree to us coming up?

His hair is white and his eyebrows white too, white as frost, and he has a moustache, stamped like sticking plaster under his nose, bristly and sharp. His eyes fix us coldly. Maybe not cold, but thin, if you can say that about eyes. They don't seem to have a colour at all. His hand opening the door is mottled, though the fingers are long and fine, rather like an elderly lady's. I don't know why I think that. I don't like him.

Jimmy and I exchange looks. Is he really going to tell us anything? Jimmy touches my shoulder. 'He never had a love affair with nobody,' he whispers.

The hall is wide and cold and dark. Heavy curtains remain half drawn across the windows. We follow him down a passage to the right. 'Not a very summery day, is it?' Mr Vine snaps this back at us over his shoulder as if he partly blames us for the change in the weather. Neither Jimmy nor I answer. 'In here. My study.'

This is a small room, quite light, looking out over the back garden which might have been beautiful once. A wide terrace leads down to an untidy rose garden and beyond that there are paths and a pond, but it all looks shabby now – the terrace knotted with weeds, the steps cracked, the roses wild and scraggy. The room itself is cosy enough, though everything in it – the chairs, the rug on the floor, even the books lining the walls – all look faded. 'My sanctum. Now sit down, why don't you. Sit. Here.'

We sit. He folds himself neatly into the chair behind the desk, takes out a fountain pen and a sheet of paper, lays the pen along the top of the paper as if it were a spoon, then looks up and says, 'Well, what do you want to know?'

In my view the only thing to do when you don't know where to begin is to look businesslike and start. I pull out my notebook and pencil and say the first thing that comes into my head. 'What's that?'

'I beg your pardon?'

'That.' I point to the long metal and spring thing at the foot of his desk. A monstrous black metal jaw. With teeth like you could never imagine – grey and long and so cruel they could bite you to the heart. I can hardly take my eyes from it.

'It's a trap,' says Jimmy.

Mr Vine gives a coldly approving smile. 'Exactly. Very special and not legal now.' He pauses. 'Unfortunately.'

'You used to trap rabbits and deer and things with that!' It's big enough to snap an elephant!

'Oh no.' He turns his attention to Jim. 'You know about these things, do you?'

Jimmy nods. 'My dad told me. It were for poachers and trespassers and such like. A man would lose his leg in one of them.'

'And you would like to use these things still, in Old Wood?' I can just imagine the moaning and crying of children and gypsies and badgers, all lying trapped, their legs and paws snapped in those metal jaws. What kind of a person could possibly want that?

'It was a joke.'

I don't think it was at all.

'I've poached on your land,' says Jimmy.

Isn't he great? I try to kick him but he ignores me. Why on earth did he have to say that? Mr Vine will throw us out on our ears now.

'And my dad before me.'

I sigh loudly.

'And his father before him?'

'Likely.'

'Name?'

'Flint.'

Vine nods. 'It has always been the way. Deer, pheasant, rabbit.' I can hardly believe my ears. I look at one then the other, both serious, Vine nodding slightly, Jimmy arms folded, head on one side. I know about poaching; it's stealing, sort of.

'I never went after no deer.'

'No, but it still happens. Need organization for that. Crossbow, sharp knives for gutting, know how much the deer carcass weighs, dead weight, van, contacts. There's money in that.' He laughs, more like barks, and rearranges his pad and inkstand. 'Now.' It is an invitation for me to continue and so I start again asking him about the wood and the gypsies, and Jimmy joins in. He seems to warm a little to Jimmy, maybe because he can tell Jimmy knows about animals and things, and is local. He barely looks at me at all.

We find out all the facts and figures we need. How long his family have owned the wood, how big it used to be, the number of foresters his family used to employ and all that sort of thing. We don't ask him about the Forge and the dead girl, his sister, straight off. I think we were just a bit nervous and now, while Jim is telling him about our project and how we spend so much time there at that pool, he almost becomes a different man. Almost.

'I used to play there all the time as a child with my sister. The two of us.'

Peter and Kathy, of course.

'Was her name Katherine?'

'Yes. She didn't like Katherine though – said it was too still. We called her Kathy.'

So I was right. I glance at Jimmy, trying to catch his eye. He pretends not to notice.

Mr Vine seems to unbend a little. The sticking-plaster moustache hitches up a millimetre. I think it's a smile but I am not betting any money on it. 'Nanny took us there first, for a picnic. She didn't like it very much because of the ants, I seem to remember, but we loved it. My sister was older. You call it the Forge? You do? Yes. Interesting. We gave it that name. Don't expect you've seen the inside of a forge, no of course not. Nothing like that pool, but we called it that because . . .' He stops and we wait and I wonder whether he will tell us that this is where his sister died, murdered by the gypsy girl whom he hasn't mentioned yet either. My eyes drift back to the mantrap. Did Nanny, driven berserk with the ants skittling about inside her baggy knickers, run into its metal jaw, and bleed to death before the children could fetch help?

Mr Vine's brow has deep lines on it and he is staring down on to the desk, at his hands. Such long fingers. I don't know why but they make me think of aristocrats in satin coats, and the French Revolution . . . I don't suppose Mr Vine ever had to work, not with fine hands like he has. They're good for nothing apart from playing cards, or paying bills, or strangling someone. Perhaps he was the one who murdered his sister?

I wish I didn't get thoughts like this. It makes me so sad, completely, like being dunked in sadness so I can hardly think, except of Peter. I practically have to shake myself like a dog.

I look at Mr Vine, sitting there, old and neatly pressed. He could never have murdered anyone, it would have been too . . . I don't know . . . untidy, I suppose. I think he's almost forgotten we're here. Old people do that. I give Jimmy a look and he raises his eyebrows.

'Why did you and your sister call it the Forge?' I ask.

'What? Oh, one of my sister's notions. She was like that. Odd ideas, you know. She thought it was a special place where friendships were forged. It was special.'

'And she died there?'

'Yes. You know that, do you? Everyone knows that. The Vine girl. Haunts it, poor thing. That's what the village all say, or said. Course she doesn't, not at all.' He paused. 'It's this place she haunts.' I can't quite tell if he's being serious or not. 'Damn good reason to get out.'

'You're selling up everything 'cause of her?' Jimmy sounds incredulous. 'But that were all those years ago. And you'd let it all go now?'

'There are other reasons, young Flint, other reasons.' He picks up the pencil, puts it down, moves it a fraction with the tip of one finger. Touches the ink well. His hands seem to move the whole time.

'Was she very lovely?'

'Interested, are you?' I nod and he stands up suddenly, once more all thin and sharp angles. He reminds me of a compass. His legs don't seem to bend when he walks. 'I will show you something. Very quickly and then,' he takes out a round watch from his waistcoat, 'you can go.'

He leads us back through to the hall and then up the stairs to the first floor. What a huge place it is for one person, and shabby too. The carpet is threadbare and there are long dark stains blotching down the walls of the upstairs corridor. We pass three doors, all shut, and then he takes out a bunch of keys and opens up a room, the last on the right. Five rooms just on this end of the corridor, and there are stairs going up to a third floor!

'Do you use all the house?'

'No. Downstairs. I have my corner of the house and Matthews, my . . . er . . . major-domo,' he gives one of his barking laughs, 'he has his corner. The rest of the old pile is gradually going to hell if you must know.' I wonder if he thinks about Uncle John in the same way as I do. 'Don't have much need to come up here, except to this room.'

He pushes open the door. 'You asked me about my sister. That's her, over there. Just as she was.' For half a second I expect to see Kathy Vine sitting in a rocking chair, or the ghost of her; he had said she haunted the place. But there's no one there. Jimmy edges in in front of me and I follow him. It's a nursery, pale blue walls, a brown chest over by the windows, shelves with tin soldiers, ranked up and marching out towards the edge, and above them a row of diaries. At least I think they are – some could be old, tatty exercise books, but I think they are diaries because there's a child's desk by the window and that has one of the exercise books open on it. When Jimmy and I wander over and I pick it up, he practically bites my head off.

'Leave it alone! I said you could look, not pry.'

'Sorry.' But I have seen what's written on the cover in bold black print: 'Kathy Vine's Secret Book' and then at the bottom of the cover in smaller round handwriting: 'Katherine Vine, Aged 8 years 5 months'. It makes me feel strange, just for a moment, seeing her name, written by her there in front of me. I put the book back carefully and give him my I-really-didn't-mean-to-it-was-an-accident look and he nods and clears his throat.

'Private. I . . . look at them sometimes.'

I can understand that. I wouldn't want him or anyone looking at my diaries.

Facing a narrow black fireplace is a sagging sofa lined with bears and dolls in yellowing lace, and then a piano and over that a large painting out of which stare two children, a boy and a girl. Of course, that's what he meant when he said, 'That's her.'

'She and I.'

So that's her. I don't know whether it's what I imagined her to look like or not. The picture is so strong, unlike anyone I have ever seen. Her eyes are wide and dark as pools of water, and her skin is pale moonlight, that's right, exactly, moonlight. She is everything and he is nothing beside her, the boy, holding himself stiffly and looking down at her because she is sitting. I get the impression that the artist had only been interested in her. Perhaps it is the slight tilt of her head, or the look in those dark eyes, almost defiant, challenging the painter perhaps, though heaven knows to do what – flick paint at her probably.

'A year before she died. And she said she was dying even then. But she always said things like that, for effect, or to frighten me.' Again that dry laugh.

I am aware of Jimmy moving up beside me. What had he been looking at with such interest – the old teddy bear? I glance at him but he's gazing up at the painting as if it's the most important thing he's ever seen. I think he's acting but I can't say anything. '*Was* she dying?' he asks.

'Mm?' Mr Vine is miles away, somewhere in the painting, staring up at her and, this is the odd thing, rasping his hands together. I don't think he knows he's doing it, just rubbing them together as if he were washing and washing them.

'Dying.'

'Certainly not. Always did what she wanted. You can see it, can't you?'

Yes I can, and she doesn't look as if she's dying to me, looks more alive, in an odd way, than anyone you might see walking down the high street.

A phone begins to ring somewhere downstairs. 'That's it,' he says, all clipped again. 'Out you go.'

*

On the front step, Jimmy is standing in a bit of a funny way with his hands behind his back. For a moment it makes me wonder whether he's hiding something. 'You oughtn't to sell up, you know,' he says. 'You oughtn't to do it.' Which is what I wanted to say but didn't feel I could, and then I forgot. I don't think Jimmy forgets anything. I edge back to peer at what he's holding in his hands, but all he's doing is tucking his shirt in.

Mr Vine stands thin and stiff in the half-closed gap of the door, the dark shadow of the hall behind him. 'I don't think it's your business, young man, what I do.'

'Maybe.' He always surprises me the way he can do this – talk his way round adults. He does it to Miss Tracy and my mother and now to Mr Vine who, instead of shutting us out as I'm sure he wants to, opens the door a margin wider. Jimmy's not being cocky or sticking out his chin like he's looking for a fight, but . . . well . . . as if he's giving advice to someone he's known all his life. Weird how he gets his ears pulled and booted out to stand in the corridor one day and then can act more grown-up than a grown-up the next. 'Maybe, but your family and this village go back a long way, don't they?'

'Yes.'

'Hope you don't mind me sayin' so, but don't you care about the wood being cut down, and the village changed, and the gypsies driven off? Don't you mind all that?'

Mr Vine has begun his secret hand washing again. First the long fingers of one hand and then those of the other. 'Everything comes to an end, Flint. My sister used to say that. The house will go. And the wood will go. And the village will change. And that is the way things are. After a bit no one will know or care that a family called Vine lived up here. Or, indeed, that a family called Flint used to poach in their woods. Now off you go, the both of you.'

'Yes, of course, right-o.' He turns away and then, as if he has just remembered, he turns back again. I know what he's up to, he's play acting. He's being so polite, if he had a hat he would be twisting it around in his hands or tugging his forelock like they do in the old stories and his voice has become suddenly more fuzzy and burry, more like the way Miss Green talks. 'One last thing, Mr Vine, and 'scuse me for asking – who was it your sister made friends with down at the Forge pool in the wood? Was it someone called Molly Birkin? Do you remember her? The wood keeper's girl, I think my dad says she was. Was it her?'

'Yes.'

'Did your sister promise to give her the wood or something like that? Because that's what I have been told, that the wood isn't yours to sell anyroad. Is there any truth in that, Mr Vine?'

I tug Jimmy's sleeve. I think Mr Vine's rather a sad figure, and I think Jimmy's pushing it. I want to leave.

'No. If you bothered to do your research properly, Flint, you would know that the girl, whom my sister befriended – befriended, I may say, against the wishes of my entire family –' rasp rasp go his hands, 'was no good. In fact she –'

'I know,' interrupts Jimmy, more like his old self now, less bothered about being polite, 'killed her dad.' Mr Vine's head jerks, as if he's been stung on the nose. 'But that was because he beat her, that's what they say. Do you know why he beat her, Mr Vine, until she went so crazy she turned on him?'

'How should I know what went on in that family? The girl was always mad! Now go away.' And he tries to shut the door but Jimmy sticks his foot in the way. I grab his arm and give it a yank but he shrugs me off. I really didn't know he could be this hard.

'If the wood's hers, why won't you let her have it? It's thieving not to, whatever she did.'

'To her? Whatever she did? Do you really want to know what she did?' His voice is cold and quavering with barely-controlled anger. 'She killed my sister.' Jimmy, taken by surprise I think, steps back and Mr Vine snaps the front door shut, but I see his face, and though I don't like him – he isn't the sort of man anyone could like – I see the pain there, and I feel a bit sorry for him.

'You hurt him,' I say.

'I reckon he's lying through his teeth.'

Jimmy's like one of those dogs; when he gets hold of something he won't let go. On and on.

'It's only what I told you. Molly did murder his sister.' I don't mean to sound smug but I probably do a little bit. I like being right.

'Yeah, but you just make things up; this is real. And I'm going to prove him a liar too. I can.' His face is hard, flinty; there's white under the freckles. I can't think why he's like this, why it means so much to him. I thought I knew him: I'm not so sure now.

I can hear the phone ringing again. We get the bikes and walk them down the drive. I don't think Mr Vine is as bad as Jimmy is making him out to be. It's funny, it's almost as if he's seen a different man to me. I just think he's sad; dried up like a cheese cracker. He didn't *have* to show us that room but I know why he did – he wanted to share a bit of his childhood, to show us his sister. I would love to show Peter off if I could.

But when I say this, Jimmy pulls a face like he wants to spit. 'He's unhealthy.'

'Don't be silly.'

'Sitting up in that room. Reading those diaries. Course he is and I bet it were his family had Molly beaten, bet they did. And he were part of it. I bet. People like him make me sick.'

He's making me cross. 'Worse than your brother?'

'No.' He avoids looking at me. 'But just like him. Anyway I got plans for him and all.'

'Oh? What plans are they?'

He shrugs.

'Well, what do we do now? You can't prove he's lying, can you?'

'I'll find her, won't I? She'll tell.'

'But she's mad.'

'No worse than him. Are you on his side then?'

This is stupid. 'Go and see her then,' I snap. 'Just watch out she doesn't strangle you, or poison you, or whatever it is that she does.'

'All right.' And he gets up on to his bike and pedals fast, and I'm left standing there, watching him go. Why is he doing this? Has he found out something, or done something he doesn't want to tell me about?

I look back at the sullen house and then get on my own bike.

The day has lifted and the air is thick and musky against my face as I free wheel down the long hill to the village. My mind keeps going back to the pool, and how it has already swallowed more than poor Kathy Vine. Mr Vine has been swallowed too, except he doesn't know it and he thinks he will be free by selling. And the way Molly hangs around by it all the time, maybe she's trapped too. You can be drowned and not dead. I think of the metal jaws of the mantrap and I think of Jimmy. Perhaps he is waiting for me the other side of the gates.

CHAPTER SIXTEEN

Jimmy didn't wait for me at all; off down the hill as fast as he could go, bike waggling like a duck's tail as he stood on the pedals. Couldn't wait to get away, and that's it.

I let the slope take me, free wheeling, slowly gathering speed, trying not to use brakes. Don't ask me why, but I got a sudden notion that I wanted to smell my own breath. Have you ever tried that, on a bicycle going down a hill? I nearly killed myself.

As I reach my house, Mum appears at the garage door. She squats down, sticking her paintbrush crossways in her mouth while she rummages in her overalls for cigarettes. 'How did you get on?'

I tell her about Mr Vine and she says people who are rich shouldn't be sad. Perhaps she has a point.

'Where's James?'

'We're not married, you know.'

She gives me one of her 'odd' looks and then sort of coughs and laughs at the same time, and, when she's got the tar in her lungs all settled, says, 'Kate, I've been thinking, you know.'

'Oh?'

'About something you said.'

This is a change.

'I'm going to hand in my notice.'

'Give up your job?'

'Yes.'

It doesn't sound much does it? But I can hardly tell you what it makes me feel. At times like this, other families rush around and hug each other, at least they do on the telly. 'That's great, Mum,' I say. I wish I was one of those cartoon figures whose eyes can spin round and flash messages. 'Have you told him?'

'Not yet.' She gives me a quick smile. 'I've been given some contacts in Hereford. There's a restaurant wants a mural painted. What do you think?'

'More pigs?'

She laughs and looks pleased. 'As a matter of fact, yes. I'm going to have to go in tonight. Do you mind?'

She means do I mind being left here on my own. I would, actually, quite like to be taken into a restaurant in Hereford but I know we can't afford anything at the moment.

'Of course I don't. And then quite why I ask this I don't know but I say, 'You're not thinking of marrying anyone, are you?'

She doesn't bite my head off. Come to think of it she hasn't bitten my head off for a couple of days now. 'Have you anyone else in mind?'

'Mr Smallwood is nice.'

'Who's he?'

'The priest.'

She laughs again and runs her hand through her hair. I wouldn't mind a laugh like hers, when she's not coughing, that is; it's warmer than a hot water bottle. She stands up and stretches and, before disappearing into her den, gives me a little pat on the cheek, well, more a stroke really. 'I'll be off in half an hour. You can make a sandwich and watch TV.'

'OK.'

I feel my cheek.

I spend the rest of the day working on the project but it's hard to concentrate. In the middle of a sentence I find myself stuck, staring out of the window at the wood, dark and green and secret, and I have to shake myself. I even turn my back on the window, but I feel the wood there all the time, waiting. Can a wood know anything?

Of course that's stupid, but I just wonder whether places soak up something of the people who live and love and die in them. I read an explanation of ghosts that was something like that. A person feels something so strongly – a terrible love or fear usually – and the place where they have that feeling acts a bit like a tape recorder or a film camera perhaps and records the moment. And then from time to time, other people coming along set off that recording and see a ghost of the person who had loved or feared, reliving that tiny bit of their lives over and over.

There's at least one ghost in that wood, down at the Forge. That's not what I mean though. Sometimes, like now, the wood is like a creature, not just trees, but one creature, and all it does is wait and grow and feel. Maybe what I am feeling now are its thoughts reaching out to me. It can't be too happy if it's figured out that it's about to be chopped down.

Mum's evening was obviously a success because when I got up on the Sunday she was already in the garage working on endless rough sketches for her mural. And then with more apologies, she's off from lunchtime till late. Uncle John phoned once, said he was just touching base, whatever that means.

There's not a squeak from Jimmy. I got up early to catch him delivering the papers but it was a boy I'd never seen before.

Wednesday. This is the third day he's been away. I don't like to look at Miss Tracy when she does the register. He's going to be in such trouble when he does turn up, and yet I can't go round to his place – I can't, not with his brother there.

Not long now till the end of term and my birthday. Mum keeps asking me whether I want a party. I don't know. I had hoped maybe Jimmy could come round but there's no point in saying that when I don't know what has happened to him.

At the end of school yesterday, Miss Tracy tried to

catch my eye but I pretended not to notice and hurried out with a whole bunch of the class, deep in conversation with fat Simon. Actually it wasn't deep conversation at all; I was quietly threatening to squash him flatter than a rat-skin rug if he made one more joke about my 'missing boyfriend'. He makes me sick.

Anyhow, I'm not Jimmy's keeper. We don't have any special arrangements, not really, only the project which I felt was a bit more than a project for both of us. It was. It is.

He can do what he wants. I won't stop him. And I certainly won't go to his house looking for him.

I went to the newsagent's this morning on my way to school. There was an old man talking to Miss Green about the gypsies and how there was to be a meeting or something. I didn't pay too much attention. I bought a two-p. chew because that's all the money I had, and I asked Miss Green about Jim. She was very sorry in her dithery sort of way and said that her brother had given away Jimmy's job because he was no longer reliable, turning up too late for his rounds, or not even turning up at all.

Am I the sort of person who can only have one friend at a time? Some people must be like that, I suppose. Am I starting to be friends with Mum?

And now I keep remembering the bruises down his arm; dark purple blood under the skin, pinched, punched or trapped in a door . . . Supposing something bad has happened to him . . .

After lunch I heard the Head talking to Miss Tracy. 'I'm sorry, Sally,' he was saying. I never would've believed her name was Sally. I never think of teachers having names like ordinary people. 'I'm sorry, but we have a legal obligation. We must bring in the Social Services.' I turned away, a sick feeling in my stomach. Nobody should be allowed to be taken away and put in a home if they don't want to go. Nobody should be taken away.

I forget about the business of the meeting about the gypsies until Mum comes home with a copy of the local paper. Mr Smallwood has arranged it for Sunday in the village hall. She says Uncle John is furious. He believes the gypsies have deliberately tried to sabotage his development and that the priest is meddling. She laughs. 'I told him he sounded like King Henry.'

'What did he do?'

'Murdered Thomas à Becket, his Archbishop.'

'Oh. Did Uncle John find that funny?'

'Not really.'

'I like Mr Smallwood,' I say.

She smiles. 'I know you do.' Then, 'I think we should go to the meeting.'

She's in a funny mood so I don't know whether to take her seriously or not. Anyway I can't think the meeting will do the gypsies much good. Nobody in my class is at all interested in them, certainly not in the sense of being concerned about their homes.

Everybody reckons they are responsible for the recent robberies.

'Won't Uncle John be cross with you?'

'John,' she says, kicking off her neat-heeled shoes so hard that they fly up and over Jimmy's flower bed, 'can look out for himself.' I don't know what she means. Then, without bothering to change out of her suit, she disappears into the garage.

That was an hour ago. I don't disturb her when she's working; and she doesn't disturb me. It's one of our unspoken agreements.

She went in looking like one person – her office self, the one that she's tried to construct since we moved down here, all colour coordinated and efficient, with the exception of the stockinged feet of course – she emerges looking eye-blisteringly brilliant – paint splattered everywhere. She marches in, puts on the kettle, and then with her hands on her hips says, 'Well, I've done it.'

'The painting?'

'Handed in my notice.'

'You told him on the phone?'

'Of course. I don't want to be anybody's secretary again. I don't want to wait on the end of the phone ever again. I don't want to receive anyone's charity ever again. That's what I told him.'

I am impressed. 'You said all that? Just like that?'

'Well, no, not exactly. A bit friendlier I suppose.'

'You're different.'

She thinks about this. 'Am I? Yes, I am. I have to say you've made me think, and so's Antoinette. She was horrified when I told her . . .'

Antoinette, it seems, is the woman running the restaurant who's as crazy as our butcher about Mum's pigs. We'll have to change our name to Porkie. Isn't that another word for lying? Mum mentions her a lot now – Antoinette says this, says that. I begin to picture her – seven foot tall with an outsize spoon in one hand and a fat-bladed chopping knife in the other: Ms Genghis Khan. She can't be too bad, though, if she persuades Mum to do what I've been wanting her to do for weeks.

The next morning, just as I'm walking out of the front door for school, Jimmy turns up.

'Come on,' he says, like he's not been away.

What would you do? Ignore him? Walk past him? I nearly do. Friends should never disappear like he did, but what I say is, 'How was Mars?'

'What?' There are black rings under his eyes, his T-shirt is stained with dirt and green, and one of his trainers has bust open at the side. He's a mess, but tipping up and down on his toes with excitement. 'Oh yeah, I was busy. I got something to show you, come on.'

'Right now?'

'Yes.'

I've never skipped school before. God knows what

Mum'll say, or Miss Tracy. They'll skin me. But I hardly have time to worry because Jimmy is hurrying me so much. We cut into the wood our normal way, but head north up past the Forge, following the stream up hill. Quite steep the path, and I am hot and out of breath by the time Jimmy grabs my arm and stops me. 'Here.'

'What? Where?' For a second I can't think what he is talking about. We're not really even in a clearing. There's a heavy bank of green – rhododendrons. I can hear the stream close by us still and then I realize I am looking straight at a hut, tucked in between a tree and bushes. Shaped like a capital A, the sides woven with green, tight as a mat.

'What do you think?'

'You made it? On your own? No help?'

'It's good, isn't it?'

It's better than good.

I peer inside. The ground is dry, sandy and smooth. There's a mat and a little stool and hooks under a plank shelf with a white mug and tin plate at one end, and a kettle at the other and a blanket folded on the stool. It's neat as a ship's cabin.

This is what he's been up to. Forget everything. Forget friends. Forget school, and work in the wood building a camp. Did I tell him it was my birthday soon?

'Is it for me?'

'Don't be stupid, Geoff. It's for her.'

CHAPTER SEVENTEEN

For her! For the old woman!

'Well?' He's up and down on his toes, cocking his head to one side, checking the back wall to see whether the branches are snug, knowing that I have to be impressed but wanting to hear me say it.

'Why make it for her?'

'Wha'?'

'I don't see why we can't leave her alone. Mr Vine said she killed his sister. Mr Smallwood said she poisoned her father. I don't see why you have to build her a hut.' I sound pretty reasonable to me.

'Mr Vine said –' says Jimmy, mimicking me.

'And Mr Smallwood.'

'He don't know everything.'

'And you do?'

He falters for a second. 'My dad has told me things, and she's told me things and all. Molly wouldn't hurt nobody. Not now.'

'Jimmy, she poisoned her father.' I'm having trouble getting the message through to him.

'Yeah, she did –'

'See.'

'But you don't know what he did to her. Perhaps

she didn't have no choice, Geoff. You make people do terrible things if you hurt them enough.'

'Mr Vine said . . .'

I think I probably would've gone on like that for ages, *tick tock, tick tock*, because I was thinking about me, and she frightens me and I think in a way I didn't want to know anymore about her. I had the story in my mind and I didn't want to change it, but Jimmy just keeps on doggedly explaining.

'Some people don't care about other people at all. You know that, Geoff, come on! I expect your Mr Masterson's like that, isn't he? Just smash stuff up that's in his way, yeah? Just like with the gypsy camp.'

'Maybe.'

'And I tell you there are some worse than him. What about Frank? See what he done.' He pulls up his T-shirt and shows me another angry black bruise, and there's still the old mark on his arm.

'Jimmy!'

He shrugs. 'He likes hurting people, does our Frank . . . and what if her dad were worse than our Frank? That's what my dad says he were like, beat her so she could hardly walk.'

All I can see is his horrible bruise. I reach out and touch it; it's hard. 'Doesn't your dad do anything about Frank?'

'Nah. He's Dad's angel. Frank has something of my Mum's looks. He'd never believe nothing bad about him.' He pauses and tucks in his T-shirt. 'I

wouldn't tell him anyway, it would kill him, I reckon.'
He squats down and scoops the dry mould from the
forest floor and lets it run through his fingers. I squat
down beside him. 'D'you see what I'm saying now?
There's those like Frank and then there's people like
Molly. They're the ones that get smashed up an' hurt
an' broken.'

'And you?'

'Me? I don't get broken; but I don't forget nothing
neither.'

'Would you poison someone?'

I can see him relax slightly. He smiles. 'Don't be
daft.' Then something catches his attention off to the
right and he holds up his hand to stop me saying
anything. 'She's here.'

'Here?'

'Don't look – it'll frighten her off.'

'I thought you were best friends.' I don't mean to
sound sour.

'She's gone nervous since they smashed up the old
cottage.'

I'm getting a crick in my neck from not turning to
look, and she there watching us. Unless he's having
me on. 'Are you having me on?'

'No. I think it were Masterson, or his men, looking
for her, or for something she might have hidden. Wait
here.'

He walks unhurriedly across the clearing and then
she steps out from the green of the wood and stands,

uncertain, it looks like to me, waiting for him. I can hear him talking quietly, reassuring. 'It's all right, Molly. You remember, Kate, the girl. You know.'

She doesn't look so wild nor so witch-like as before and she keeps her face turned to Jimmy and has a hold of his hand. The plastic shopping bag that she always seems to carry is still with her.

When they come up to me, she looks at me strangely, perhaps trying to see the other girl she had first taken me for. She makes me think of a stray animal. Her face is dark from being outdoors and from dirt, so are her hands and thick black nails, and there's a sharp smell off her that almost makes me back off, but I don't.

All she says is my name, just the once and then listens while Jimmy talks to her, telling her about me, about Mr Vine, about the supplies he'll get for her from Mrs Smith because she's promised to keep helping.

I don't want to be left out. 'I can bring some food,' I say.

'That'd be a help,' says Jimmy, 'wouldn't it, Molly?'

Her face lightens for a moment then she turns away from us and, stooping a little, enters the hut.

We gather wood for an evening fire for her and Jimmy tells me how he has spent the days since our visit up to the Vine house. He went right into the gypsy camp and talked to Mrs Smith. It was she who told him that they couldn't keep Molly safe much longer. Masterson's men were at them every day. It was then he found out that they had levelled the cottage. 'But not before they had gone through it with a comb, that's what she said. They're OK, the families there, they really are. It's not them does the thieving.'

'How do you know?'

'I just do, all right?'

It's like a challenge. I don't know why he should get steamed up over this, but I'm not going to fight. 'OK.'

'Mrs Smith is a good woman, I reckon, but they don't have much hope of staying put. All this will go.' He nods to the hut. 'Her too and all.'

It's so quiet here, I can only just hear the stream and that faint breathing of the trees. It's as if there's only the two of us, three of us, in all the world and it's hard to believe it won't stay like this for ever.

'It's not fair. This is hers by rights,' Jimmy says.

'You still believe that?'

'I reckon Masterton do 'n' all. What else were his men looking for in that old cottage but papers? You know, legal stuff. Wouldn't do for there to be another owner of the wood if he wants to build all over it; but she's too wise for that. I reckon she got her papers hidden somewhere else.'

'Have you asked her?'

'She won't say nothing about it. Clams right up.' I can believe that; her middle name is probably Clam.

Molly Clam. I've never heard her say anything apart from our names: me and Peter that is. 'You know where she's got it hid? I reckon in that bag of hers.'

'Have you looked?'

'She won't let me near it.'

I remember him when I first met him – wild and noisy, and pinching sweets in the shop – and now he won't even peek into a plastic shopping bag. Has he changed or is this what he was always like and I didn't see?

I did bring food the next day after school, and though she wouldn't talk, or couldn't, not with me anyhow, she seemed not so shy. She made me a little crown of wild flowers when I brought her the food, and it was only sandwiches I brought – peanut butter and cucumber. She was clean too. Jimmy was there. I think he sleeps up there. He's not in school anyhow. His brother called round to our house wanting to know if he were with us. Mum said no and shut the door in his face. She asked me if Jimmy was all right and I said he was. She seemed happy with that. I'll tell her everything, but not just yet.

It was Jimmy who washed her. He took her to the stream and washed her feet, helped her out of her clothes. She didn't seem to mind the cold, he said. I can't imagine him washing her, but he did.

That evening, Uncle John called round. He was in the house when I came back from visiting. Mum had given him a drink but he wasn't drinking it. They had obviously 'had words' before I came in because Mum was being coldly polite, not the way she ever used to be with him.

'So here's the little girl, then.' Not his usual greeting. I begin to retreat.

'Just a word, Kate.'

I don't know what he wants to say but whatever it is I don't think I want to hear it. Why hasn't he gone abroad? He said he was going. Mum gives me a searching look. I raise my eyebrows and shrug. What has he found out?

'No, don't leave the room.'

I feel guilty. I don't have anything to feel guilty about. I haven't done anything. I wonder whether he's as bad as Jimmy said he was, that he'll smash to get what he wants and he'll hurt whoever gets in his way. Dad didn't last long working with him, that's for sure.

'You and your friend visited Mr Vine, didn't you?' I nod. 'Well, since your visit he's discovered that some property, highly personal property, has gone missing. Do you understand? Things of his have been pinched. My friend, Peter Vine,' he says, 'has had some stuff pinched from the house. A little thing but personal, you know what I mean?' I know what he means. He means Jimmy. What has Jimmy done? If Mum thinks either of us stole anything from anywhere, she'll never speak to me again. Never. She'll hate me. 'You don't know anything about it do you, Kate?' I feel very cold and still but I say absolutely nothing. And I won't either.

I don't have to, Mum replies. She is very cross and it's with him that she's cross, not me – at least not yet. 'What are you getting at, John, are you saying –'

'I'm not saying anything, am I Kate? Just that he told me he would call the police unless his things were returned. It was something precious to him. A book I think it was.'

A book? One of the journals from the nursery! Once again I see Jimmy and the odd way he behaved. I thought he had had something behind his back – out of sight, sneaking it from the shelf.

'Are you sure you don't know anything?'

'Of course she doesn't know anything. Up you go, Kate.'

My face is blank as a brick wall but I hope not as red.

I can hear angry words between them and him saying, 'All right. All right.' And then immediately after that just his growling about the meeting that's been called in the village hall. 'That vicar . . .' he was saying, 'stirring things up.' Good for Mr Smallwood.

It can't have been more than five minutes later that I hear the door bang and then watch him crossing the garden to the gate.

I only have three precious things: my picture of Peter, Rabbit and my journal. I don't know what I'd do if someone stole any of them.

Is Jimmy a thief?

CHAPTER EIGHTEEN

I couldn't think about anything else. Had he really stolen one of those journals? He had. Was he still pinching things from sweet shops then? Would he grow up to be a thief like whoever it was who was breaking into the houses in Bexstead? I couldn't help remembering how neatly he had slipped in through the back window of Molly's cottage. Could I really have misjudged him so badly?

I knew I would find him in the clearing where he had made the hut, and I was all steamed up for another row.

He didn't even try to deny what he had done. Yes, he had pinched the journal from the playroom. Yes, with me almost standing beside him!

I hated to hear it. And I hated the way he had made me a part of it – and I hated having been so stupid not noticing. 'You're a lying thief!' I shouted, which was a bit rich really because he hadn't lied about anything but I was hardly listening to what I was saying I was so upset.

'Don't you ever call me that,' he said so sharply that for a second I thought he was going to hit me. I don't know what would have happened, World War

Three most likely. It would certainly have been the end of everything. I'm not like him, the way he can forget stuff like that. I can't. Anyway he didn't hit me and I suddenly heard me the way he must have been hearing me and it made me think of Mum and Dad, so I shut up.

He said, 'He's the thief, Geoff, you read the journal and you'll see. I knew he were lying and I could see that all them books were written by his sister and that they would have to tell the story about this place and I were right. I got it here, look.' He disappeared into the hut and came out a second later with one of the hardbacked exercise books I had seen lined up on the shelves in Kathy's room. 'I were going to tell you. I were . . . but I knew you'd be cross.'

I took it and said, 'You still shouldn't have pinched anything.'

'And do nothing? Yeah? Go on and read that. Go on, then you can tell me what I shouldn't've done. All right?'

I read it from the first page right the way through with him reading over my shoulder. Normally I hate that, the sound of someone breathing in my ear when I'm reading but all I heard was Kathy Vine's voice.

June 23rd 1919

They won't let me see her. They won't let me go down to the wood. They want to keep me in this room, in this bed until I wither and die. This, I think, is worse than the sanitarium in Ladimonte. At least there I could breathe, I could see the mountains and the clean, clean snow and I felt then that life was worth struggling for. Here there is only my poor, poor darling Molly and they won't let her up here and they won't let me down to her. When Peter comes home from school he will talk to Mama and Papa and make them change their minds. How I hate being so weak.

The handwriting was bold with sweeping, extravagant flourishes and splodges where in her anger or excitement she had pressed too hard and the nib had splayed.

July 19th

I was up today at the very crack of dawn (how like the very 'crack of doom' that sounds — and perhaps that is where I am standing), up and out of my vile bed. I could walk easily to the window and I stood there, looking down over the wood, towards the Forge and Molly and I remembered how we played and played and how Peter was always with us. My shadow.

I stood by the window for two whole hours, the sun shining on me and my skin looked translucent. I felt so full of sunlight I thought I could float away —

it's this stupid illness that makes my skin so thin. If
you do prick me, will I not bleed?

Nanny was very cross. I was too tired to shout at
her and slept through till lunch.

Peter came back yesterday and I am full of hope.

July 20th

I hate him! He is worse than all the others because
he knows how much I love her and is jealous. School
has turned him into a wretched, spiteful young man.
His heart has shrivelled. He makes me think of winter
and sharp frosts. I hope he lives in his winter for ever.

This page was heavily thumbed and I wondered
whether this was the particular journal that haunted
Mr Vine. She described how he came to see her in
her room and how he had stood there stiffly, hands
clasped behind his back. In his view her tuberculosis
was a blessing because it kept her from that gypsy
girl. Their friendship was *'unsuitable'*, *'inappropri-*
ate', *'shameful'*. She had scored two lines under that
last word.

He was no longer her *'pet'*, her *'shadow'*, but *'that*
traitor'. She herself became *'the prisoner'* and her
parents, the icy, unloving *'gaolers'*. *'Both Mama and*
Papa,' she wrote, *'seem to me colder and more remote*
than those snow-peaked mountains I used to gaze at
through my window at Ladimonte.'

Her friend was her kindly nanny. Through her she twice managed to smuggle messages down to Molly.

July 24th

The only one I shall miss when I escape from this dismal place is her, my sweet thing. Dear Nanny, she has seen me writing in this and yet she never pries. These are my precious secrets, my real life. Only here can I be me.

She dreamed of escape. Practically on every page she wrote that she was feeling stronger. '*I have so much life bursting in me that sometimes I wonder why it is that I cannot simply spread my arms and fly out of this cage.*' She forced herself out of bed and walked up and down her room. '*I managed three turns today and felt only a little faint,*' she recorded. Perhaps she did become stronger, for her bouts of exercise became longer and longer until finally I came upon the exultant entry: '*Triumph!*' For the very first time since her return from the sanatorium, she left the room, crept down the narrow back stairs used only by the servants and '*in the pale moonlight*' crossed the lawn and walked a little way down the hill towards her wood and then, too tired to go on, stood gazing at it, remembering. '*It is so much a part of me, it is like my heart.*'

The wood is mine, my property, even Papa cannot take it away from me. I have written to Mr Screed and said that I wish to make a will. They cannot stop me doing that either. Only Molly loves this place as much as I and she shall have it when I die.

A week later, after an angry exchange with her brother, Mr Screed was shown into her room and '*the wretched business*' of drawing up a will was accomplished.

From this point on, however, she seemed to lose heart. Her entry for the 25th August was long and sad. Even her handwriting was changed, the loops thinner, the letters sometimes shakily formed, and all the wild splodges and exclamations gone. Yet it should have been another triumph for her since, not only had she managed to escape again, but she had also reached the wood, and met Molly.

My heart ached to see her so badly hurt. She limped to meet me at the Forge, her pretty cheek swollen, her dark eye closed to an ugly squint. Had I the strength, I would kill him with my own hands. I would. Each night I pray for his death.

The 'him' was Molly's tyrant father, a poacher turned wood keeper. He had beaten his own wife into an early grave, and he beat Molly too. *'He is an evil, evil man, but he will never crush her, never take her from me.'* They talked and held each other and the wood shielded them for a little while from *'the harsh prying world'*. All Kathy's concerns were for her friend, and yet that entry, for the very first time, clearly showed that she knew she only had a few months to live.

She made her plans. The two of them would run away. *'And,'* she wrote, *'when I die, Molly will have everything that belongs to me, then she will be free for ever.'*

The very last entry is dated:

3rd September

Everything is ready. What little money I have is transferred to Coutts Bank in London. That is where we will go. No one will find us there.

I have said my farewell to Nanny. Poor dear, she would not talk to me but I have told her to take my journals and burn them. I know she will. I think she understands that my love is not wicked. Molly is my true sister though we come from two different walks of life. My last months will be with her.

And those were the last words. What could have happened? Kathy had died, had drowned in the pool but Molly had never killed her as Mr Vine had claimed. How could she? Jimmy was right. Vine had lied. 'Free

187

for ever.' What a sad and terrible thing. Molly had spent her life locked away, every bit as much the prisoner as Kathy herself had been.

Jimmy and I talked for a long time trying to decide what to do. It was his idea to make a copy of the journal because, much as I didn't want to see Mr Vine again, I still felt we must take the journal back to him. I felt sure a newspaper would be interested in the story. Wouldn't they be moved to fight for Molly and see that she wasn't cheated out of this gift? I persuaded him to give it a try though he wasn't that keen; he still wants to look in her bag where he is sure she keeps a will or something that proves the place is hers. But he won't unless she lets him.

My namesake was right, the wood is beautiful and I think I do love it too: the Forge, the sandy hill with the badger sett, the endless stream, and this sunlight blinking down at us through the leaves. And I think knowing that it will all go makes the love dig deeper into me, so that it hurts. Everything precious is fragile and can easily be lost, like Peter.

CHAPTER NINETEEN

It's Saturday afternoon and Mum is taking me into Hereford for a treat; she is going to take me to the restaurant where she's been painting the mural, her next commission. The owner, Antoinette, wants to introduce her to lots of other people who will shower Mum with work. Mum's been paid and she says she's rich now. Mum always says she's rich when her purse is full so I don't feel too guilty asking for a bit of spending money. I need quite a lot to photocopy the journal which I've tucked away in my red backpack.

Mum buys herself a new pair of Levi 501s and a man in the store tries to chat her up while she's parading up and down in front of me and staring in the mirror. She completely ignores him and keeps asking me what I think. I tell her she looks brilliant which is what I know she wants me to say, but it doesn't speed up the process because she then says, 'What do you really think?' I think she rather likes having someone trying to chat her up. He's quite young; younger than her. I buy a red cap with 'The Washington Redskins' written on it with the picture of a scowly Native American Chief on the front. Mum says it suits me.

Mum's friend at the restaurant, Antoinette, is terrifying to look at: wider than a sofa and with hair that's bright flame orange and a dress that would do as a tent for Jimmy and me. Mum says she looks 'marvellous'. Antoinette never stops talking all the time we're there.

She obviously loves Mum and calls her 'my positive dream person' which is a terrible thing to call anyone but since she is as far from normal as I am from the Milky Way, I suppose it's all right. I think she is OK really but it isn't a very relaxing treat. However we do get buns, home-made ice cream, and hot chocolate with cream. She makes me try three different types of home-made ice cream. Heaven is probably made up from different types of her home-made ice cream.

The restaurant is to be called Circe. Circe was a witch who turned men into pigs. Antoinette says that all men are pigs, however her restaurant will be such a wonderful experience that it will make them human again. Mum's mural has beautiful brown ladies with slanty eyes surrounded by pigs dancing about on their hind legs balancing glasses of wine on their snouts. It's fairly odd.

While we are there a young man comes out of the kitchen. He's introduced as Danny. 'Sit down, Danny,' booms Antoinette, 'and have a coffee with us.' She turns to me. 'He is the chef, darling, but he is a hopeless man. I am going to sack him once we really get going.'

'Is she?' I ask him.

'She might,' he says. He smiles shyly at Mum and she smiles back. I think he's nice.

'Why? Aren't you any good?'

'He is fantastic, darling,' interrupts Antoinette. 'A positive poet, but he is still a pig. He will have to go.'

I think she's joking but I'm not entirely sure.

I leave Mum to go to the library to photocopy the journal. I think Antoinette is a bit stupid to call all men pigs.

On my way to the library, I go into the offices of the local paper, the *Hereford Examiner*, to find out what they are doing about the gypsies. The receptionist says they will send someone to cover the meeting but as soon as I start to tell her about Molly I can see her eyes glaze over. She interrupts me to say they did something on old people recently and thanks me in the sort of voice which is like a door shutting.

Jimmy's at the house waiting when we get back at five. Mum is all for inviting him in but we'd agreed beforehand that the journal had to be taken back that day. I offer to come with him but he says there's no point; he's going to sneak it back without being seen. I don't know how he'll manage that and I don't like to ask.

I admit that the *Hereford Examiner* wasn't interested and ask him what he thinks we should do next. 'You're always going on about the vicar, aren't you?'

he says. I'm not actually but I don't say anything. 'Why not show him the copy you made? He's holding the meeting tomorrow, isn't he? Maybe it'll make him stir things up a bit.' So that's what I do.

I cycle over to the vicarage and tell Mr Smallwood the story and then produce the copy of the journal. 'It's all right,' I assure him. 'It's not stolen or anything. I promise you.' The journal isn't stolen any more, is it? 'Mr Vine has all the originals.' I glance at my watch – Jimmy should have had it back by now so I'm not lying.

'Very well,' he says, 'but I think we won't talk about this. Is that agreed? To no one.' I nod. 'And I won't enquire as to how this copy came into your hands. Agreed?' I nod again. 'Goodbye then. I'll see you at the meeting.'

The village hall is packed. There are some of the children from school but it's mostly adults. I recognize some from the school gates. There's a table on a raised platform at one end. Mr Smallwood's up there, and beside him sits Uncle John, smiling.

Jimmy and Mum and I are halfway down the hall and seated to the right. The meeting doesn't start on time. Mr Smallwood keeps looking at his watch and then down towards the door.

'Waiting on Mrs Smith to turn up,' says Jimmy.

I see Frank and a couple of heavy-looking men leaning against the wall on the far side of the hall.

Finally Mr Smallwood raps a hammer down on the table and begins the meeting. He explains that this is an opportunity to discuss not just what is going to happen to Old Wood but to the whole future of the village. Uncle John outlines his proposals which, of course, he makes sound wonderful, if you like words such as 'facilities' and 'shopping areas', 'malls' and stuff like that. And he reads a statement from Mr Vine which says the Vine family haven't been able to manage the wood properly for years and that perhaps the time has come to make a 'realistic' – that was his word – 'use of the area'. The people all listen politely.

A bank manager welcomes Uncle John, which is peculiar because there isn't a bank in Bexstead, and says his ideas are splendid. Uncle John smiles and looks completely at ease.

I look at Mum and she's frowning. 'Say something,' I hiss at her.

'I can't. Not yet.'

'Why not?'

'We're new and . . . we can't, not yet.'

It would be a real slap in the face to Uncle John if she were the first to speak. I find myself wishing she would. Slap him in the face, I mean.

In fact it's little, slightly-deaf Miss Green from the newsagent's who speaks first. She likes the way things are and doesn't want houses squashing the old village into the ground. One or two others support her, Miss Tracy is one, and a fair old discussion gets going. It's all very polite but no one, it seems, is going to mention the gypsy families and what's to happen to them.

It's only gradually that I become aware of the noise above the chatter of voices in the hall. It's the sound of car horns, and a drum banging, and then something like a fiddle playing. Mr Smallwood looks towards the door, and then a man down at the end of the hall actually opens the doors. 'It's them gypsies,' he shouts, 'and loads more an' all.'

It's quite a sight. There's a battered old lorry painted red, blue and gold, with a banner declaring 'The Romany Right to Live', and at least six more cars and vans trailing behind, all moving at the speed of the walkers – the gypsy families, babies and all – who are headed by a grim-faced Mrs Smith. There are some New Agers in there with paint on their faces, long scarves and beads. They're the ones with the drum and the fiddle. They look great.

Mr Smallwood welcomes Mrs Smith up on to the platform. Uncle John stands up to shake her hand but she ignores him and from then on the meeting gets noisy. Mrs Smith has a hard time making herself heard. There's a crowd barracking and chanting 'Gypoes out!' And others trying to shut them up, and Jimmy yelling, 'Listen to her, will you!' I glimpse Frank smiling quietly to himself up against the wall. People are shouting and shaking their fists. Scuffles begin. I see the large gypsy with the earring, the one who chased us off that first time we'd sneaked to the camp, shouldering his way through and grabbing one of Frank's pals by the shoulder and swinging him round.

I can feel Mum all tensed up beside me. 'Kate, we must go. Tell Jimmy.' I have no intention of going.

Then Uncle John's on his feet and he roars so loudly he manages to quieten the hall down. I have to admit I'm impressed. 'It's quite simple,' he growls. 'My friend, Mr Vine, and his family have owned that wood for hundreds of years. He is selling the wood to me. So I will own it. I don't think much can be simpler than that. As a matter of courtesy to your vicar and you, I have outlined my plans and shown you how you will all benefit.'

Mrs Smith looks stonily ahead, saying nothing.

'All the permissions from the council and planning committees were granted to Mr Vine years ago and my bulldozers are moving in tomorrow. As far as I am concerned that's it.'

So it's finished. I suppose I knew it was always going to end up like this, with Uncle John getting his way. I think about my view from the window, watching the sun roll down behind the wood like a golden old penny; seeing the rooks' black wings almost creaking in the evening stillness as they go back to their nests. I think about the glade with Molly, that'll end up at some stage as a neat little garden. And the Forge, where I'd have liked to live for ever, what'll that be? A drain perhaps, levelled and buried.

'Thank you, Mr Masterson,' says the vicar. He's the only one who appears unruffled by the whole thing. 'I think Mr Masterson is right that, sadly, little more can be achieved at this meeting, but at least everyone has had a chance to get to hear what the issues are. Mrs Smith?'

'This won't be the end of it,' she says. 'The travelling people are always being pushed and shoved about. We have been here for generations too, and there's never been bad feeling until this man,' here she points at Uncle John, 'moved in and started tearing the place apart. I know what people are saying, but there are no criminals in my families. If you have problems in the village look somewhere else for the guilty parties. Wouldn't you agree, Mr Masterson?' Uncle John shakes his head and smiles as if he is saying she is right off her trolley. 'Lastly, we don't believe Mr Vine has any right to sell the wood. We don't believe it is his to sell and we won't give up the fight.'

Mr Smallwood stands up. I thought he was just going to send us all home but what he actually says takes me by surprise. 'I have listened to all of you. Some of what I have heard has shocked me –'

'Get on with it, vicar.'

Perhaps the owner of the voice had wanted to be anonymous but Mr Smallwood is no sheep. 'You!' he thunders, pointing his hand and coming right to the edge of the stage. Heads turn, people move sideways to avoid being the one pointed at by him. 'You! Come out where we can see you.' It's like a sea parting, and there's Frank lounging against the wall, arms folded, smiling quietly. 'Voices in the dark. Rumours and accusations. That's how you tear a place down, not with bulldozers and crowbars, but by fear and suspicion, prejudice and violence. I'll not have it.' He pauses. There's complete silence in the hall. 'Have you anything good or useful to say?'

For all his cool, Jimmy's brother has no answer. He just turns his back on the priest and unhurriedly walks towards the door. People move aside to let him go.

'Are there any more of you who would like to walk out now?' Nobody moves. I look at Uncle John and he's scowling. None of this was what he had expected. It seems to me that he's on the point of saying the same thing as Frank, and maybe he does because Mr Smallwood looks sharply towards him, waits a moment and then shrugs slightly and addresses us all again. 'Before I close this meeting, I would like Mr Masterson to confirm once again that he will soon be the rightful owner of Old Wood. However, before he does so I must reveal that I have certain proof that suggests that our friend Mrs Smith is being badly wronged, and that Mr Vine has no right to sell what is not his. I believe the wood was bequeathed to someone outside the family, and I believe that Mr Masterson and Mr Vine know this.'

Uncle John a crook! That's what it sounds like. There is a stir as people crane to see how Uncle John will take this. He is smiling but I can tell he's raging. He snaps his briefcase shut. 'I shall see my lawyers, Vicar,' he says. 'Thank you very much.' Uncle John stands up and without a glance in our direction, he leaves by the side door. And that's it. The crowd pour out buzzing with talk, there's revving of cars, the lorries pulling away, and groups making for the pubs. Mum and I say goodnight to Jimmy and head home.

Just before we turn off for the estate, Uncle John's Mercedes pulls up beside us. Mum and I stop and the car's window whispers down. Mum doesn't say anything and nor does he for a moment. His face is oddly lit by the light on his dashboard.

'Are you getting in?'

'No, we'll walk, thank you.' Mum's grip on my arm tightens, a warning for me to keep my mouth shut.

'What did you think of that for a farce?'

I can smell drink on his breath.

Mum doesn't answer.

'Well, well, it's nice to know who your friends are . . .' He seems to notice me for the first time. 'You and your pal pinched that book and gave it to the priest, didn't you? A girl's diary . . .' His laugh is sour like his breath. 'Now there'll be lawyers –'

'What do you want, John?'

'Not a thing, Megs. Not a thing. My mistake.' And the window begins to whisper up again as the car pulls away. We stand watching the tail lights disappear into the darkness. Mum lets out her breath and I suddenly realize how tense she was. She puts her arm round my shoulder and we walk home together. I feel so tired.

CHAPTER TWENTY

It's begun. Jimmy said it would start at first light and he was right. 'Early bird gets the worm.' I feel like a worm, lying in this dewy grass at the edge of the trees, spying at the file of yellow bulldozers moving out from the site across the road and now spreading into a ragged line down in the paddock between the road and the pitch with the four remaining caravans. They must have suspected it was going to happen today too. I can see one of the young gypsies standing guard with what looks like a baseball bat in his hand. What good's a baseball bat against a bulldozer?

I knew Uncle John wouldn't waste any more time, not after the meeting, and Jimmy said Frank let slip that 'the heavy beetle crushers' were going to 'do the business' today. I hate the words Frank uses.

The guard is yelling and clanging on a pot, families are tumbling out. There doesn't look to be more than six or seven men there, all of them clutching sticks or bats or spades. I thought that some of those hippy New Agers who'd rolled in for the demonstration might have pitched in, but there's no sign of them.

I can't help being here, at the end. If it was the end of the world I'd have to get myself up into a good place: a mountain or the Eiffel Tower or somewhere to get a view. Jimmy came with me through the wood but he wouldn't stay. He's gone to the hut to see Molly's safe.

The bulldozers have smashed through the old fence. The one at the far end of the line is actually at the edge of the wood and has started to grind into it. There's a screech of wood tearing and a tree is down, like yanking out teeth. If he keeps going I'll be flattened like one of those cartoon cats after they've been slammed behind a door. But they'll not catch me. I'm going to watch it all, and write it down. Even if it's stuck in one of my diaries like poor Kathy Vine's journals, somebody might read it and know what happened today. It's not much, is it? Better than a baseball bat perhaps, but I don't know. I wish . . .

There's no point in wishing. How silly it seems now, me being a witch so that I could change everything. Nothing could change this, not unless I were the fifteen metre tall giant woman of Bexstead-under-Wood. There's a thought, I could pick up the bulldozers and use them as ear plugs.

The machines have ground to a halt in a kind of semicircle around the four caravans. They've lowered their shovel thing but they seem to be waiting for a signal to begin. Is this the last chance? There's hardly a gap to let the caravans through; they can't mean to smash them, and with all the children there!

I can see Mrs Smith on the step of her van, mobile

phone in her hand, shouting away, and a handful of gypsy men around one of the nearest machines, banging on it, kicking it, one of them scrabbling up to the cab to get at the driver. The next machine along rumbles straight for the nearest caravan. There are screams. I see the driver who's under attack swing something black and heavy, I don't know, a wrench or jack or something and the gypsy flailing back on to the ground, and another scream as the caterpillar track catches part of him. I can't see; his hand or foot. Oh God. This is not a cartoon, this is real but I can't tear my eyes from it. The other men half drag their injured friend back out of the way, but meanwhile the claw of the semicircle has tightened. An old woman spills out of the first caravan as the bulldozer begins to trundle it along the rough ground, juddering and tipping it. And now it's gone! On its side. Please don't let there be anyone else in it. And the bulldozer is grinding up and over it. Disgusting. Crunching it down as if it were an empty Coke can.

The families are milling about, frantic now, pulling possessions from the three remaining caravans: TV, bedding, pots. What's the point? They're going to lose everything.

And then about a million things seem to happen at the same time: I hear crashing in the undergrowth behind me and Jimmy yelling my name; I see a dark blue truck pulling off the road and coming more slowly across the rough ground towards us; and Mrs

Smith trying to push and shove her families together – perhaps she thinks they'll be safer like that, or more easily squashed. I don't know, but she's not being successful and I can hardly think straight or see straight because my eyes are blurred and I'm aching inside and I'm up on my feet and running, straight for that old woman who'd tumbled out of the now flattened caravan and who's wandering helplessly in front of those machines.

I hear Jimmy yelling my name and then I have my arms round her. Poor Molly. Poor, poor Molly. So frightened she doesn't know what is happening except that perhaps she has walked into hell. Poor Molly. And then Jimmy is on the other side of her and I don't know how but we have her through all the screaming and yelling and into the temporary safety of the wood's edge.

Jimmy's scratched and torn and out of breath and I can't talk, there's a pain in my side like the bite of Mr Vine's mantraps. I wish he'd been lying in his bed under the first of those metal crabs.

Molly has one hand against a tree, leaning her weight on it, bent slightly, breathing quickly, little shallow breaths, and looking back down at what had been the camp.

I can't tell exactly what's happened, but the line of machines has certainly come to a halt. The blue van has spilled out a camera crew, and Mrs Smith seems to have reined her families in together.

Jimmy and I head back past the Forge and up towards the glade and her hut, and all the time I'm thinking she can't stay there for ever. There is no for ever anymore. If they don't tear up all the wood this summer, the summer itself will end, and she can't survive a winter out here. I don't think Jimmy has thought of this.

Not that she's doddery and frail, not really. The grip of her hand around mine is hard and tight, and she can walk quickly and quietly, and she's walking all right now, her face hard, her mouth a thin line. I've not seen her like this before. But she *is* old and much of the time she's sort of lost in herself – that's how Jimmy describes her. We can't look after her, not every day through the winter; not that we've talked about it, but we can't. I know that.

Jimmy is cursing. 'They could'a killed someone, some of the kids, you know. They got no right. They got no right!'

There isn't too much point in talking to him.

When we get to the glade, Molly goes straight into her hut without a word to either of us. Jimmy slumps down while I root out the kettle. I can't think of anything more useful to do than get some water from the stream and make a cup of tea.

'Here!'

It's Molly, standing at her makeshift door, the precious plastic bag in one hand and a yellowy envelope thrust out towards us in the other. 'Here.' I think it

204

hurts her to talk, something physical, in her throat. Probably never talked in her hospital for the last forty years. She is angry too.

Jimmy looks up. He can be up and down like a yoyo, Jimmy. His face brightens with excitement and he jumps up and practically snatches the letter from her.

'Careful,' I warn him, sounding just like Mum, 'you don't want to scrunch it.'

We read it together. It's exactly what Jimmy had said it would be: direct proof that Katherine Vine left the wood to Molly. We could stop everything. Just like that.

. . . I have written to the lawyers but I don't know whether Papa will allow me to see them on my own. If they come, I shall make them write out everything in such a way that no one can change this gift of the wood which I give freely and wholly from my heart to you, my very dearest friend . . .

'Can we take it? Can we?'

Molly dips her head, but her eyes are on the letter which I now have in my hands.

'I'll look after it, I promise, and see you get it back.'

'Where're we going to take it?'

'Mr Smallwood, of course. He'll know what to do.'

We run. We run all the way through the wood. My guts ache so much I think I'm going to be sick, but I run. Every minute counts. Every second. I run harder than I've ever run before and I keep up with Jimmy every step of the way back to my house where we grab the bikes – there's no sign of Mum – and then race up the road to the vicarage.

Jimmy bangs the knocker and when Mr Smallwood opens the door I want to hoot out our triumph, but I'm still so out of breath and so's Jimmy that, even though we try to explain, he can't follow what we're on about. It's not till he's shown us into his little parlour and has the letter in his hand that it finally dawns on him, but instead of cheering he frowns. I don't understand why he doesn't seem more delighted. I know he's on our side; he made that plain at the meeting. More than that, he actually said that he believed that Mr Vine had no right to the wood, so he obviously believed the journal.

'This is the same writing as in the journal?' he says, looking up at us over his narrow reading glasses.

'Yes.'

'It's proof, isn't it?' says Jimmy. 'You going to phone someone straight away, are you?'

'Yes, yes,' he says, but in such a way that alarm bells begin to ping inside me.

'What's wrong?'

'I shall telephone Mervin, Screed and Pike. I found out that they were Mr Vine's family solicitors, though I don't know how helpful they will be.'

'But what's wrong? Isn't this the proof we need to

get everything back to the way it should be with Molly as owner of the wood?'

He folds the letter and carefully slips it back into its envelope. 'It might be. Unfortunately, I believe that for it to be legal, it would need to have been witnessed. She could have had her nanny witness it, but . . . well . . . as it stands I don't know. And there is one other thing.'

'What's that?' Jimmy sounds like I feel — flatter than a squashed rat. The letter is like the journal. It tells us the truth but it isn't any good. It won't help change anything. Jimmy is right: people like Mr Vine and Uncle John always get what they want in the end.'

'You know where Molly Birkin is, don't you?'

'Of course,' I say glumly. 'She's living in the wood. Jimmy made a shelter —' and then I 'ouch!' as Jimmy kicks me. He knows what's coming. I don't think I'd see a train even if it came smacking through the living-room door straight towards me.

'She'll have to go back into the hospital. She can't stay out. She really can't.'

'Why?'

He sighed. 'For one thing, I've discovered she needs an official release form before she can leave that hospital. She was committed there — you know that, don't you? — after the death of her father. She was considered dangerous. I know we don't think she is, but for the moment I do believe she is best there.' He hesitates. I can see he is debating as to whether to tell us something else.

'And?'

'I think that after that meeting, there might be some other parties interested in finding Miss Birkin . . .'

Jimmy's on his feet and moving for the door and I jump up to join him. I know what's going through his mind. We should never have left her, not alone.

'I'll see what the lawyers say,' Mr Smallwood calls out after us. 'And I shall phone the hospital too. They'll send an ambulance.'

'Hospital will kill her,' Jimmy shouts back at me as we cycle back down the lane and then on to the road to the estate.

It might. What I hate is the thought of Uncle John's men finding her on her own, and there being no one there to speak for her.

CHAPTER TWENTY-ONE

She's not there.

The kettle is where I left it on a flat stone by the unmade fire, the door to her hut is ajar, the little washing line that Jimmy had strung up is bare.

We crash into the clearing like a couple of wild heifers and then stand stock still.

'Molly?'

'They've already got her,' says Jimmy.

In the background, behind the sound of the stream, I can make out the rumble of those machines working again.

'One of us should have stayed.' He sounds drained.

'Yes.'

The way she looked when she handed the letter to us, did she know that it was over?

The door of the hut suddenly swings wide open. We both start forward and then stop. There's Frank sitting on her little stool looking out at us.

'Molly,' he coos. 'One of us should have stayed.'

'What you doin' here?' Jimmy's voice is steady but his face has turned pale behind the freckles.

'Looking for the old hag,' he says pleasantly. 'Seems like everyone's looking for her. Pity I didn't find her, the boss would have been pleased and it would have been worth a few bob.'

'You'd sell your mother!' I snap.

'What? Got a tongue, has she?' He jumps up and in two steps is out of the hut and has my hair yanked back so my face is tipped up to his. 'Then maybe you can tell me where she is?'

I don't care if I go bald, I clench my fists and eyes and bite my tongue.

'Leave it, Frank!' Jimmy's calm has gone and I can hear a shake in his voice.

'Well?'

I lash out and connect with his shin; I was aiming higher. He yanks again and then suddenly lets go so I fall flat on my back just as Jimmy launches himself at Frank from the side. But he's too late and I see it all as if it's happening in slow motion: Frank, still smiling, stepping back and then his arm in a leisurely swing that catches Jimmy right smack on the side of his face.

The momentum of his charge still carries him forwards but off balance, keeling sideways. Frank steps in and cuffs him, like a bear might, across the back of his head. Jimmy drops down on to his knees. I scrabble up and run towards him but too late to stop Frank kicking his younger brother in the stomach. I've never seen anything so deliberate in my life. Jimmy crumples into a ball, waiting for the next kick.

'Stop it! Leave him alone.' And not knowing what else to do, I do the same as I dream so many times that I'm doing for Peter, I throw myself in front of him, wrapping my arms around him, waiting for the thump of his boot in my back.

But it never comes.

'Oh,' says Frank, as if pleasantly surprised, 'that's sweet, that is.'

I look up at him and I hate him and I curse him silently, wishing him all the most terrible things I can think.

'I think the old hag got something hidden here, hasn't she?' he says. It's as if nothing has happened. 'Couldn't see nothing inside, though. The boss said it would be a will, you know, long bit of paper with writing on it. Course you do, eh? Did she show you something like that?'

He throws her few meagre possessions one by one out through the door of the hut, while I cradle Jimmy. His face is swelling, and his lip is cracked. He opens his eyes. I help him to sit up.

'Nice hut. Nicely made. You got quite a talent, Jimmy lad.' He's working at the door, testing it. 'So you got nothing you can tell me?'

'You've done it, Frank. Don't expect nothing from me ever again.'

'Oh, is that right?' With a sudden wrench, off comes the door. Then he takes the door jamb and slowly twists it around and as he does so the whole structure begins to twist and shift, and as the frame of the door collapses, the hut sags. 'There we are,' he says brightly, moving round the distorted remains, kicking as he goes. 'That finishes that.'

Jimmy has levered himself to his knees. I take his arm and slowly get him to his feet.

'Now you can tell me where you think she might be.'

'I don't know,' I say.

He shakes his head. 'Don't believe you.'

'Back off, Frank.'

'What?'

'Back off or I'll kill you.' Jimmy has a knife in his hand, a pocket knife, but the blade glints sharply and Jimmy doesn't sound like himself at all, but someone older and harder, someone who will do exactly as he says. 'Leave us alone, Frank, all right?'

Frank looks at the hand holding the knife and then at Jimmy, his eyes narrowing a fraction, judging what to do. But I think he hears in Jimmy what I hear, and suddenly he shrugs and turns away, walking off in the direction of the Forge and the camp, whistling. He gives the kettle a kick that sends it scuttering along the ground, and then without turning back at all, he's swallowed by the trees.

Neither of us say anything. We head in the opposite direction. One of Jimmy's legs has gone dead so he has to lean on me and I sort of put my arm around him, to hold him steady.

'I know where she's gone,' I say. 'Up to Vine's.'

'Yeah. I reckon she might.'

We concentrate on walking – hobbling in Jimmy's case – back to my house. I am praying Mum is there and will help us out. If she's not around, we'll never get up the hill, not him anyhow.

Luckily she's back from Hereford and when she sees us coming through the garden gate and sees what a state Jimmy is in, she doesn't go into one of her wild flying panics but takes him into the kitchen straight away and bathes his face and listens without shouting at me, listens to everything I say. The letter, what Mr Smallwood said, Frank and what we now have to do, which is to reach Molly before she gets to Mr Vine.

'Will she kill him? What'll she do?'

'What can she do?' says Jimmy bitterly. 'She's like us, isn't she? It's what they'll do to her. They'll say she's dangerous, they'll lie and have her locked away for ever. That or kill her.'

There's no pleading or argument, Mum bundles us both in the car and drives us through the village and up the hill so fast that my hands are gripping the dashboard the whole time.

We're no more than a couple of minutes too late.

As we swing in through the gates, the first thing I see is Molly's black clad figure, hurrying across to the door. And when Mum actually pulls up, the door's open and Mr Vine and Molly are facing each other.

None of us move, not for a heartbeat, then I shove open the door and get out.

What was it? Sixty years since they had last seen each other? More than that since they'd played together down at the stream, Peter Vine tagging along with the two older girls, idolizing Kathy, maybe idolizing them both, but then getting jealous. He's dried up now. A stick insect. Jimmy was right. He had lied. Molly could never have killed Kathy. Never in a million years. He'd lied and then robbed poor Molly of her life.

They're like statues, the two of them. Mr Vine is holding the door in one hand as if only too anxious to close it again. 'Who are you?' he says. 'What do you want?' But he knows who she is, and he looks frightened. She says nothing, just gazes at him.

I'm half aware of someone else in the background, talking into a telephone. Afterwards I wondered whether it was Uncle John but there was no sign of his car.

Mr Vine tries to shut the door in her face. 'Go away.' His voice quivers.

I don't quite remember how I acted or what I said. I thought I asked Mr Vine what he'd done, whether he knew what he'd done. Mum told me later that I was screaming and sobbing, which I find hard to believe. Jimmy just says I was wild and that I threw it all at him: how Molly loved his sister and how could he do such terrible things to this girl, this woman, who had been his friend? And he knew all along what he had done, sitting up in his room, reading her diaries, knowing. And then trying to say she, Molly, was a killer.

Old Mr Vine just stood there, trembling. I do remember him saying one thing. It wasn't so much to me as to her. 'It hurts,' he said. 'The past hurts.'

I don't believe that. I do not believe it. Not any more. It's now that hurts.

And then Molly spoke. 'You and your family.' I remember this clearly. 'You killed her,' she said. 'And you kill her again by stealing Old Wood.' Her voice was so rusty and quiet the sound of the police car sweeping up the gravel drive drowned out her words to everyone but me and him.

She didn't say anything after that, not even when the two police officers, one of them a police woman, gently took her and guided her into the back of their car.

CHAPTER TWENTY-TWO

It's all over. At least that's the way it seems. The end of Molly, of the gypsy camp, of Uncle John's plans, and it's the end of term. I handed in the project. It wasn't half as good as I'd wanted it to be but then Jimmy hardly did any of it at the end. I should have realized that that would have been the case. Not that it seems important at all now. Anyway, I'm more concerned for Jimmy; he's behaving really oddly, completely withdrawn. Even Mum has noticed. He spends most of his time, I think, down in the wood. I don't know what he's up to, watching the machines maybe.

You know, they did televise the gypsies being 'evicted'. We watched it on Uncle John's television that evening. I thought maybe having the telly people there might have stopped Uncle John's men. It didn't. There was no sign of the caravan-crushing though.

The next morning, I took Mum down there and the machines were at work, scrawing up the land, turning everything level and dirty and brown. There was a stinger of an article in the *Hereford Examiner*, and there were pictures too but I don't expect that will change anything. I won't go down there anymore.

And now it's Saturday and my birthday. Mum

asked me what I wanted to do today and I said to visit Molly. I didn't think she'd agree. She hates hospitals but she said, 'Of course we can, if that's what you want.' So that's what we're doing. 'Would you like James to come too?'

I'm watching her dress. She tries on a black cotton jacket and turns sideways to look at herself in the mirror. She always does this, perhaps she thinks she will disappear like a playing card.

'What do you think?'

'Perhaps not.'

'You're right, I don't need it today. It's going to be warm again.' And she slips it off. In fact I was talking about Jimmy. I hoped he would have called round by now. He knows it's my birthday, I reminded him yesterday as we were coming out of school. But he hasn't even phoned.

'Just the two of us then.' She smiles. 'Is there anything we should take her?'

I had already gathered some wild flowers from this edge of the wood. I'd made a tiny posie of eyebright, something that would fit in an egg cup, and also a circlet, a little crown it was meant to be, a bit wonky but I thought she might like it. She'd made me one once. I show them to Mum.

'Will they last?' She touches the tip of the crown. 'So delicate.'

'No, not for long.'

*

I'd been looking forward to my birthday for so long, it should have been wonderful, like in the films – laughing and celebrating and funny hats. I think it was one of the saddest days of my life; and what happened right at the end when I should have been asleep, in bed, a whole year older, having sweet dreams, was worse; that was a nightmare.

It was only when we were standing in front of the hospital gates that I remembered that I had seen it once before, on our drive down. That seemed like a long time ago now. I had even held up Rabbit so that he could look at the cold grey building himself.

The hospital was right in the middle of town, Martyr Lane. It wasn't a lane at all but one of those nothing sort of roads – offices, closed-down shops, thin houses, the odd newsagent, and then this tall black grilled gate flanked by walls the colour of ash. It was a fine day but I had the feeling the sun never shone here.

Mum had phoned to check whether we would be all right to visit, so we had no problem going through security. A man with a face that looked like mutton chops made us sign a book and that was it.

It wasn't horrible inside but sad somehow, not a place you wanted to talk in and certainly not a place you would expect to hear laughter. A young woman in starched white escorted us up a green tiled stairway to the third floor; there were no lifts in the building. 'Always considered too expensive to install,' she said.

Then we went along a corridor, all green and cream, even the light there had a faintly green tinge, as if it were partially under water. As we walked along we heard the murmur of voices, and once heard someone calling. The only constant sound though was the clack of our feet on the hard floor.

'You have a maximum of fifteen minutes,' she said with an efficient but not unfriendly smile, unlocking the door to the last room on that corridor. And then she was off – a bit like the white rabbit in *Alice in Wonderland*, I thought.

If the whole building had an air of sadness, this room was the heart of that feeling. It was small – one window, with a chair beside it, that looked out onto a tiny rectangle of tired grass with a solitary tree in the middle. There was a pale-blue bird's egg in a neat round nest on the edge of the window sill. Had Jimmy been to see her already, and without telling me?

A threadbare rug lay across part of the rust-red lino floor, and opposite the door was a black iron-frame bed. Molly lay on the bed, her back to us.

'Hello, Molly,' said Mum softly. 'I've brought a visitor for you.' And she touched her arm.

Molly shifted slightly and turned her head in our direction. She didn't seem to see Mum at all, only me. 'Kathy,' she said, her voice more of a hoarse and rusty whisper than ever.

I placed my silly crown beside her where she could see it and the little posie of eyebright too – and I suddenly wished I hadn't done the crown, but she looked at it for a long time and then slowly she took it up in one of her large brown hands, then placed it on her forehead. 'A girl,' she said.

Mum looked about to cry. She stroked the back of Molly's head and bit her lip.

'Shall we come again?' I said.

She took my wrist. 'Kathy.' Her grip was so strong, it felt as if my bones would crack. 'My wood,' she said. 'You and the boy.'

'What?'

'It's yours.'

If only it were hers to give away.

'Poor thing,' I heard Mum murmur softly to herself.

She let go my hand and turned her head away towards the wall.

'Goodbye,' we both said, but she made no response.

Mum had planned to take me to the restaurant again, but neither of us were in the mood. Mum knows the whole story now and when I get the copy of the journal back from Mr Smallwood I'm going to give it to her to read. She asked me if there was anything I wanted from the shops because my real present wouldn't be ready for a couple of weeks. I didn't want anything. I think maybe she is painting me something. I hope so.

As soon as we were home, Mum was on the phone

to the director of the hospital, demanding that Molly be given a better room and firing a whole string of questions about the legality of keeping someone like Molly under lock and key for so long. Could she be released? What kind of care would be provided for her if she were? Did they hold any private documents, wills and such like relating to any property she might hold?

We had talked about the cottage that had been demolished, surely that belonged to her, and obviously Mum was half hoping there might be something in the hospital safe that showed that the wood was hers after all. I could hear a kind of sputtering buzz at the other end of the line as Mum grimaced and held the earpiece away. She waved at me for her cigarettes which I passed to her. 'Oh, so I'm not the first to ask about her papers. Can you tell me who else . . . No, I'm a friend of hers and I'm, er . . .'

'Going to tell her story,' I hissed.

'Yes, I shall be documenting her story. The BBC have expressed interest . . . Oh, Mr Vine had enquired. When was that? . . . Several weeks ago, I see. Thank you.' She put the phone down. 'Well, I don't know how much good that will do. But you were right, Kate, you really were. Mr Vine obviously believed that the wood wasn't his at all. The so and so, and he went and sold it anyhow. I wonder what we can do now.'

There wasn't anything. I said it was all over and it

is, but I suppose the real end will be when the wood is gone and forgotten, and Molly is dead.

I was in bed when Jimmy phoned. I didn't have a chance to get at him for forgetting my birthday, he sounded so far away and frightened. 'You know,' he said, 'that I'd plans for Frank ... Well, I got him, Geoff. I did.' He sounded like he was phoning from a hall or something, I could hear voices all the time in the background.

I felt suddenly cold and frightened. 'Where are you? What did you do, Jimmy? Jimmy ... Jimmy, are you all right?' Mum was watching me.

'I'm all right,' he said.

He didn't sound it at all. Mum took the phone from me. 'Hello, James, where are you? Where?' She looked across at me. 'The police station. I see ... don't worry at all. We'll be ten minutes, no longer, I promise you. Now put the sergeant on the line. OK. Bye ...'

I don't think I was very helpful to Mum but she convinced me that he was safe, and the very fact that he wasn't at the hospital meant that he wasn't badly hurt. But I just kept getting these awful flashes of how Frank had beaten him in the wood. If he'd ever felt that Jimmy was a real threat he would've tried to kill him.

We were only in the station two or three minutes before Jimmy was brought in to the waiting room.

He was deathly pale with a horrible strawberry bruise down the side of his jaw, and he walked funny, leaning against the policewoman who was with him. If he hadn't grinned when he saw me I think I would have howled. I really would. He came over and sat with me while Mum sorted things out.

He told me what had happened; the whole story. I should have guessed. I think I half knew most of it anyway. Frank had been doing all the thieving, making it look like the gypsies were to blame, and he had been using Jimmy, forcing him to climb in through windows. But Jimmy had got him back. He had told the police where Frank's lock-up was, where he had his stash of goods – TVs, new furniture, all sorts. Frank hadn't dreamed Jimmy would tell on him, not until the last minute when he saw the police cars pulling up. He had hit Jimmy so hard then he had half knocked him out. But the police had got him, that was the thing, got him red-handed. Frank would be sent down for ages, Jimmy said. I hoped he would be locked up for ever.

Mum was extraordinary: no hysterics or scrabbling for cigarettes, no shouting or anything. She just did all the right things, and when she was finished and Jimmy was released she offered to take him back to his dad.

Jimmy looked down at his feet. 'I'm sorry, Mrs G.,' he said, 'but I can't go back there, not for a while, I reckon. When Dad knows what I done, it'll kill him.

It will.' He sounded quite matter-of-fact. 'I knew it would be like this.'

Mum didn't hesitate. 'Then you'll come home with us and I'll speak to your father.'

CHAPTER TWENTY-THREE

So that was my birthday.

I think my real birthday happened a fortnight later, even though to begin with things still looked bad. Jimmy was charged with being an accessory – Frank had named him, of course – and so they wouldn't let him stay with us and he was put in a children's home until the trial. We visited him every day and, although he grinned and acted tough, he looked so small and dwarfed by the guards and the other boys we saw there, that I don't like to remember it.

Mum and I visited Molly too. Jimmy asked us if we would. 'Some of them do give up,' said the nurse who showed us in. 'It's sad. We try to give them an interest, but when they don't try . . .'

I think she did try. She held my hand and smiled when I chatted to her about our project on the wood. She looked so frail though. I thought she was fading away.

After that, I spent a lot of time in my room not doing anything. Mum didn't fuss me. She had her work, she was also on the phone a lot, and had endless forms that were driving her crazy. I could hear her shouting down in the kitchen. There's not a lot of point in shouting at a piece of paper but that's sometimes the way Mum gets things done.

Things began to change at the end of the first week when Mum told me that Uncle John had, as she put it, 'finally gone away on his business trip'. Disappeared off the scene was more like it. I think it's the last that any of us will see of him, and I'm not sorry. Though I suppose in his own way he has been generous to us, even if he was expecting something in return – Mum to marry him, I think.

Apparently Frank had accused him of being behind the robberies. It had all been a set up, like a campaign so that the gypsies would get blamed. Frank was meant to have hidden the stolen goods near the camp and then tip off the police. But when he found out that people believed it was the gypsies anyway, he decided he was on to a safe way of making a lot of money. Then when Uncle John wouldn't help him once he'd been arrested, he told the police everything. Of course the newspapers got hold of the story, and the next thing is that all the work on the site stops, the estate agency closes, and Uncle John is the next best thing to thin air.

Frank is facing a prison sentence – at least five years, Mum says. Jimmy won't have to go to court; he's too young, they said. There was a hearing. Mum had to go to it – she said she would have gone anyway. I didn't, because I was too nervous. Mum spoke for him, so did Miss Tracy and so did the Headmaster (which I thought was a miracle). But the fact was, Jimmy had helped Frank on a couple of occasions. He could climb through any window, no matter how small; I knew that. I'd seen him do it. They said he wasn't responsible though; Frank had made him do it. So he was let off, cleared, but there was nowhere for him to live. His father was unable to look after himself and had been taken into hospital. So Jimmy was put back into Chington House, the children's home. Mum took me to see him there, and it was a lot better than where he was before, but if he stays there he won't be coming to my school anymore.

Mum and I talked for ages after we had visited him. We talked about everything in a way that we never have done before. I discovered what all her form filling was about. She hadn't wanted to tell me earlier in case nothing would come of it. However, even before the hearing, she'd been trying to find a way for Jimmy to come and live with us permanently. There are relations of his living in Liverpool but they don't seem very interested in him at all and so, while she can't adopt him, she might be able to become a foster parent. We're keeping our fingers crossed.

And we talked about Peter. At least I did. 'Why don't you have any pictures of him in your room?' I asked.

She smiled. 'It hurt too much to start with, and then, I don't know. I just didn't want to.'

'Was it why you and Dad split up?'

'Perhaps, partly. I don't know. Neither of us managed very well then.'

And then I said what I have wanted to say for years, ever since it happened, and have never been able to. I wasn't going to but then there the words were, out in the air. 'It was my fault, wasn't it? And you and Dad blamed me, didn't you?' It made me shiver to say it.

Mum didn't nod like I thought she would. For a second, she looked as if she had been slapped and then she laughed. But it sounded like a broken laugh and she rubbed her fingers in her eyes, poking them. Then she got up and washed her face in the sink.

'You are so strange, Kate,' she said finally, wiping her face on the drying-up cloth. 'Do you know, you stare right through me sometimes? You used to make me so nervous.' I make her nervous! 'Did you really think we blamed you?'

I nodded. Of course. I should have held on to him.

'You were only seven, Kate. How could we blame you?'

'Daddy shouted at me.' I closed my eyes and I could hear him all over again. 'I told you to wait and not let go of Peter. I told you!'

'You were only seven, Kate,' she said again, putting her arms right round me. 'Only seven. It was Daddy who let you both go.'

On the Thursday of the next week, Mr Vine telephoned and asked if he could come and see us. At least he asked if he could come and speak to Mum. She said yes and made me promise to be polite. He called round at four o'clock with another man – his solicitor – a young man called John Screed, who turned out to be a junior partner of the family firm, Mervin, Screed and Pike.

Mum sat them down in the living room. Mr Screed seemed relaxed and happily accepted a cup of tea. Mr Vine, as always, looked like a stick insect – his knees pressed together, his bony chin tucked down on his chest. He let the solicitor begin the talking.

'Well, to fill you in,' he said, 'I'm sure you know my client, Mr Vine, was engaged in not only selling off part of the estate, Old Wood, but also the house and surrounding grounds too. Matters have, if you like, taken a different course, and the fact is we find that, while there was no question over the legality of the sale of the wood, Mr Vine feels that, for reasons of sentiment, he wishes the wood to go to another party.'

'Moral reason,' snapped Mr Vine, making a fussy movement with his hand. 'Not sentiment. My sister was sentimental. I am not.' He turned and addressed Mum and me for the first time. 'My father allowed a lawyer to visit Katherine, though I argued against it, and he let the lawyer, this young man's father in fact, draw up a will. But it was not a legal document because it was never witnessed. My father saw to that. And Katherine didn't know about those sort of things. Papa cheated her.' He cleared his throat. 'I'm afraid we all did. She made it clear she wanted to give the wood to her friend . . .'

'To Molly,' I said.

'Exactly. Do you have anything a little stronger than tea, Mrs Gaveston?' Mum brought him a glass of whisky. 'Thank you.'

'Do you wish me to carry on, Mr Vine?' said the solicitor.

'No.' He studied the glass in his hand and then, quite suddenly, said, 'I followed Katherine the night she died. I knew what she was planning – wormed it out of her nanny. Told Birkin, the keeper, Molly's father. Should never have done that. He was a brute of a man.'

He lapsed into silence again. The solicitor coughed politely. 'Perhaps we ought to leave this side of things,' he offered.

Mr Vine ignored him, took a sip of his drink and continued. 'They said he beat his own wife into the grave. Can't think why my father employed him.' He gave a bark of a laugh. 'Set a villain to catch a villain sort of thing, I suppose. Katherine had a suitcase. Can you imagine, sick as she was, walking out of our house in the middle of the night, with a suitcase, across the lawn, down the hill and into Old Wood? I followed her and she never knew. I followed her to the old Forge. That was where they would meet. I kept close to her in the wood, as close as I could. I kept thinking how like a ghost she looked, dressed in pale blue, and she seemed to drift through the trees ahead of me. Ironic, eh?

'We got to the Forge and suddenly she started to run. I heard the screams and whimpers too but I didn't do anything. I could only watch. Birkin had found Molly, right there on the edge of the pool, on the far side. She was down on her knees and he was battering her with a stick. How anyone could do something like that to their own child, I cannot imagine.

'I stayed hidden – spineless – did nothing to interfere. Katherine shouted out and ran up across the rocks. I don't know what happened. She must have been exhausted. She lost her footing and fell. By the time I got to her it was too late. She was drowned.'

The lady of the pool.

'All these years . . .' he began again and then hesitated, and I noticed that his hands were tightly clasped together round his glass and he seemed to be having trouble finding or forming the words he wanted. 'All these years I blamed Molly . . . Well, perhaps some good will come out of the wreckage, I don't know. I have another buyer for the house. Going to turn it into a home for the elderly. I've reserved myself a room.'

'Couldn't Molly have a room there too?'

He faced me fully for the first time, studying me. I think he found it hard to look at me to start with. I know I have this effect on some people. 'Yes,' he said, and I felt that at that moment something appeared to unlock, and his voice softened a little, 'she might quieten the ghost, mightn't she?'

I knew what he meant.

'As for Old Wood,' he continued, 'while I am happy to do what Katherine wished and pass over the wood to, er, Molly . . . only decent thing I can do, I . . . I think perhaps, John,' he said turning to the young solicitor, 'perhaps you could explain.'

'Of course. The thing is Mrs Gaveston, Molly Birkin is old, not in the best of health, and she has no family. My client, Mr Vine, is concerned that this gift of the wood is not just an empty gesture. Miss Birkin herself –'

'I don't want it chopped down,' interrupted Mr Vine, 'chopped down and developed the moment she dies. D'you see? Now that we've got it back, we want to preserve it.'

We? I glanced at Mum.

'Have you told Molly this?' she asked Mr Vine.

'Yes. Became quite animated. Funny thing was, she didn't want to accept it for herself. Wanted the children to have it.'

The children?

'Your girl, Mrs Gaveston, and that little poacher, the Flint boy.'

Us!

His voice rasped on dryly, but I couldn't take it all in and then the solicitor took over.

'But, of course, they're too young,' he said smoothly, 'so we suggested a trust to preserve and manage the wood – Birkin Wood Trust, it'll be called.'

'That sounds very sensitive,' said Mum.

The solicitor dipped his head and the tips of his ears went pink. Perhaps that had been his idea. 'Miss Birkin was insistent that the children – she meant your daughter and James Flint, should agree to choose the trustees until they themselves come of age.'

'I see,' said Mum. I'm not sure that I did but she was smiling so broadly I thought her face would split, so it had to be good news. The wood was safe and now maybe Mrs Smith and her family could keep their site on the far side. That would be something.

Mr Vine stood up, with some difficulty. Mr Screed handed my mother a brown envelope which she couldn't help looking at suspiciously. Brown envelopes, I know, mean only one thing to her. 'You can study it at your leisure, Mrs Gaveston. Telephone me if there are any problems. Goodbye.' Mr Vine didn't say goodbye, he gave us a sharp nod, waited for me to open the door and then walked out.

It was all written down and Mum went through it with me again. I like the idea of the trust. Jimmy and I will have to think very carefully who should be trustees. I want Mr Smallwood to be one; he won't let anything bad happen to the wood. I would like Mum to be the other trustee. I know she is not all that great with gardens and things but I think she'll be different with this. I'll see what Jimmy says. Then, when we're grown-up, we'll own it, and it will be a happy place, even with everything that has happened there, it will.

That was Thursday.

Today is Saturday and Jimmy's coming. All the papers that Mum was so busy with have been signed and stamped and I have a new brother – a foster brother.

And Mum has just given me my present. It is propped up on my desk and Rabbit and I are sitting in front of it.

It's a painting, one that she has been working on for weeks. Not one of her abstracts, nor one of her funny pig ones but a painting of me and Peter – him when he was four, and me when I was seven. We are in a garden with a high wall behind us. She's made us both slightly indistinct so that I know it's us but others might not, if you see what I mean. They might think it's any two children. Peter is doing a handstand and I am behind and slightly to one side of him. I didn't know what to say to Mum. I still don't. It's the most wonderful painting I have ever seen. You probably won't believe me but I've got tears streaming down my face, and I don't care at all.

There's the front door bell!